SOUTH OF THE RIVER

Poems and Stories

Brixton and Bromley Writing Groups

Cover designed by the Editor

Printed in Poland

First Printing: April 2019
Brixton and Bromley

ISBN-9781093940190

INTRODUCTION

By Raymond Little

Putting an anthology together is a long process: from initial idea to where we find ourselves now has taken thirteen months, but the roots of this project really began years before.

As any writer will tell you, getting down to the nitty gritty of pulling an idea from your imagination and turning it into something readable is a lonely process, which is why I was fortunate enough back in 2011 to attend Heather Johnston's creative writing class in Bromley after seeing a flyer in my local library. That moment changed everything. I found myself with a group of poets and writers of differing experience, each with their own unique talent, and unafraid to share their words. It is no coincidence that under Heather's guidance, and with the confidence gained from interacting with fellow writers, my first short story was published later that year.

Fast forward to the Autumn of 2017. Still a member of the Bromley group, I found myself in the Vida Walsh Centre in Brixton, awaiting the first arrivals for my own creative writing class. I had several concerns: would they take to me, and my methods? Would they be inspired to reach inside themselves, and push further than they ever imagined? Would anybody even turn up?

I needn't have worried. The nucleus of that group are still around, and the development of their already stunning creativity has been staggering. Their willingness to try new forms, experiment, and debate the nuances of how we put down in words what it means to be human has been truly inspiring. I soon began to see a quality of work that, alongside the poems and short stories from the Bromley group, deserved a readership. But this is no ordinary anthology, gathered from strangers who have never met. The fabulous work in this book is from a bunch of writers I have laughed with, eaten with, become friends with.

South of the River is a collection of the best fiction and poetry from the Brixton and Bromley creative writing groups. Some authors are already published, most will be showcasing their work here for the first time, but they all have one thing in common; a love for the written word.

Romance, history, murder, humour, ghosts, sport, drama, social comment and horror - it is all here in this fabulous collection.

SECTION I: POETRY

SECTION II: PROSE

SECTION I: POETRY

WHO DIDN'T WANT TO BE . . .

By Edna Herbert

Who didn't want to be on
This is Your Life?
I'm sure it was Wednesday
Eamonn would disguise,
And launch his surprise
On a celebrity that we knew,
When I was younger
I wanted to be on there too.

Eamonn had the red book
Engraved in gold.
The star would be in awe
As we wondered
Who'd walk through the door.
The music
Built up the pace,
And the sound of a voice
Would appear.

Then your Aunt Betsie
Says "hello darling I'm here".
It was great as Eamonn
Smiled with glee,
As you were celebrated
By your friends and family.
What stands out to me?
Was how it got everyone
That you knew.
Friends that remembered
You from the age of two.

Looking back,
You couldn't wait
For This Is Your Life to be shown again
So you could guess
Who it would be?
Wouldn't it be great?
If one day it was me.

LOCK-DOWN SKILLS

By Loraine Saacks

Have you sashayed trans the Thames to the East End of late?
No sign of Jerusalem being built there to date.
Stay south of that stream – on the shore that's secure,
The North Bank of the Thames nurtures moods you'd deplore.

Don't be conned by the columns that tell you it's trying,
To brush itself up and start gentrifying,
Don't be lured by the fancy PR crafted stuff –
There's minimal green and it's still rough and tough.

Did you ever have armed guards standing at your school door?
Did you learn 'lock-down' skills in peace time – not war?
In N16, E9 and E5's grim Parks' Loos,
Teenage footballers choose, which drugs they will use,
While the toddlers on roundabouts seek to amuse.
Unaware their play area's rife with abuse.

Don't weep too much; there's been no great change,
After seventy odd years: new era – new range.
Yesteryears' kids didn't quiver or quail,
Though ears were pierced by the night siren's wail.
Quite fun it was, dodging the V2 confetti
Now it's suicide bombers or the odd macheté.

BY THE LEMON TREE

By Samantha Edwards

I saw you,
As you stood by the lemon tree
Recalling the days long gone.
All encased in mysterious sunshine and rainy days.

Captivated by the brightness in your eyes
He held your gaze...
He wondered if this time, it would be different;
You hoped the same.

Caught up in the headiness.
You trusted,
No reason to disbelieve
That this time it would be different.
It was fresh, new and sweet...

He held your hand,
Intentional and your fears eased
But never quite left; as his hand one day would.
And yet you continued to stand.
Despite the bitter taste.

I saw you,
As you breathed in the smell of new beginnings hope filled the air,
Washing away the season of disappointment once held tightly in your hands

I watched you
As life handed you lemons
A taste unexpected and sharp
But you sipped slowly from life's cup,
And added sweet thoughts to the bitter memories creating once again...

HERO

By Ana Castellani

A dream of fame and worthy life he chose
To stand upon the throne of brave and feared
A shield of dignity, a pure blood horse
The helmet of a king

He rode, he fought, he won, and then returned
The fighting done – he went and chose his bride
They wed and they had kids and all there was
A beauty and her knight

And winter came, the hero was no more
His glory sung by minstrels at the court
For he'd been young and valiant years before
Now - memory of old.

Her Thumb is Ochre-Red

By Heather Johnston

Her thumb is ochre-red,
Smudging an arc of life on stone,
Secret, crucial. To give it soul
She breathes a wish. Lost words.

A night-bird sings at dawn. Blue! Light! Wake!
He stirs in hope, remembers, sighs,
back to reality - but dreamer, go on,
Tell your story straight, at last -

They meet awkwardly, in the park, lunch
in brown bags, full of - whatever -
not so essential. There's a new song.
That's what's important.

How can this agony endure, this is
not fair, not comprehensible, a test
That can't be passed. Words! What use -
But wordless, we can only howl.

She writes in another tongue, knows
It is untranslatable. Pretty rhymes
Or rhythms dissolve like water flowing.
And that just leaves her heart -

The girl leans from the window, whispering
Thoughts to the wind, secret and open
So maybe they can hear, so far below-
Her words tumble like doves.

We see the image, grant her wish a voice,
From thirty thousand years ago.

We hear the songbird, read the words,
Pierced by his shining thought

They exchange buns - ham for cheese - and then

Exchange old vows in new lyrics

The agony is no shorter: but
We understand it slightly more.

Her verse melts, melds, in time's chaotic shifts;
Her heart's changeless, which is enough.

Word-doves fly high across the air, no bounds
to thought, or dreams, or wishes - can you hear?

Motherhood Week 10

By Cleo Felstead

Sometimes I cry just holding you.
These are a new kind of tears
Not born of sadness or joy,
It is my empathy towards your needs
And my absolute contentedness in meeting them.

One day soon you will have forgotten all of this,
Each hug, my arms, my hold.
You will have nothing but your own heart and mind to satisfy.
And that is good.

I look in the mirror
I am disheveled
Without the time to brush my hair,
Hair that grows with the same minutes as you.
I am slow, you are a wonder of evolution.

My complexion is strained from the intense focus
Day into night.
My eyes are weary and determined,
Full of the light of motherhood.

When your heart meets mine
A universe blooms, and I say I love you.
In your drifting slumber you sigh a moan of return.

I want you to be happy
I want you to be fulfilled.
I must learn to accept that part of yours, and everyone's life, is suffering
And partly yours will be mine.
Motherhood.

Caring

By Grahame Hood

Good day, nothing broken
Bad day, tears and angry words
Demanding things I know I shouldn't give
Other days quite happy
Each in their own linked world
I do whatever needs to be done
Roughly when we agreed we would
I watch over you and keep you safe
Suggest things to do, special treats to please
Sometimes time runs away with us
But we do them the next day
Sometimes sadness comes over me like a sudden rain storm
Tears for nothing
Tears for the kindness of a stranger
But it is no life for either of us

Sometimes I think the weight will snap me
But it hasn't yet
Little triumphs please us
Like the man in the Zen story
Hanging from the cliff and bound to fall
Reaching out for the wild strawberry
How sweet it tasted!
But it is no life for either of us

Milky Way Reminds Me of My Mum

By Edna Herbert

Mum would always
Buy us a Milky Way,
And put it in the
Kitchen drawer.
I couldn't wait
To get home from school.
School uniform was
Barely taken off.
I would glide
With the Milky Way
By my side.
The blue wrapper
Had an appeal,
It was tightly sealed,
Waiting for me
To come home.
The words sang to me
As I unwrapped,
With a big grin.
Like a bride,
Waiting for her groom,
I would creep into the
The sitting room.
And eat . . .
Stuffing my face
With that Milky Way
Felt so sweet . . .
The chocolate was fluffy
It tastes so light,
As I ate through
Savouring every bite.
Look at me
Smiling with glee.
I'm so glad
For this memory, I revived
Eating that Milky Way today
I felt alive.

Whaoooooooooooooooooooo
Memories are good,
Pleasant, funny ones, too.
Mum, this poem goes out to you.

Killing Time

By Tia Fisher

I

I was killing time that summer afternoon reading your words
& fanning myself on your crumbling porch looking out over
the valley to cypress trees & sunflowers & the sound of sheep
pushed from pasture into pasture bleating & the insects humming
your fat old dog scratching its fleas all the while from inside
the sound of your harsh sleeping breaths & the whole valley
gasping sweating out a blazing summer in a shell of mountains
cupping us like a crucible as we slowly melted down the days.

I was killing time by going back in time reading the cuttings
squeezed in a scrapbook on a dust-thickened shelf squinting
at the nicotine strips of newsprint stuck in by my mother back
when she loved you enough to make those gnomic little jokes
in the margins in a spiky handwriting almost too tiny to read
& when I turned the pages each newsprint scrap was fragile
as filo pastry the crackling paper liberated from sellotape
so desiccated with age I could only wonder at how fragile
the medium had become compared to the words you typed
so long ago when you were sharp & strong & arrogant when
you were a warrior with words when I was so very young.

I was killing time during the sluggish siesta hours reading
while you snoozed & honestly I didn't want to look at you
curled up on your dog-scratched leather sofa with your arms
tucked around your chest & thinning legs so bald & naked
the surprising thatch of hair in sleep allowed to slip aside
& show a pale-skinned patch as vulnerable as a fontanelle
& I thought how maybe there could have been a summer
afternoon some fifty years ago fathoms away when you
were told to mind me & I napped in unprotected sleep &
perhaps you killed time too by conjuring these words.

II

Even if I'd listened more at school it wouldn't have helped:
what schoolchild learns this vocabulary learns the words
I need now the words I'm learning for the other end of life
soins / catheter / infection / détresse / antibiotique/ inconscient
bain de couverture / escarre/ incontinence/ démence...?

As for you just lying there dumbed propped & shrunken
on the hospital blue sheets if perhaps you've heard these
words before or understand their cruelty I cannot say
your gummy mouth just gulps & chokes at baby sounds
you act like words have never been your friends as though
you'd never nurtured them like children buttered phrases
for your bread read to me at bedtime or stopped mid-
argument to tweak my choice of barb . . . *enfoiré / pédant.*

Can you hear me Dad can I make my voice a lifebelt
reach it through the sea fog in your head pull you in
& rub you dry with words? In both languages I try
to think of clever things to say to find the *mots juste*
to fix the frays in our knotted lives & enough of them
to fill the hours & hide my anger with you for dying
for dying without words without agency for dying here
for dying here like this for taking such a killing time to die.

CONTEMPT

By Ana Castellani

Behold the righteous, fools of paradise
Their pale hands touching bibles in their trials
In demon or in god their faith disguised
The poison of a love – treason in vials.

Adorn the world in fifty shades of black
To mourn for its mischievous, empty fate
For there's no time, no space, no turning back
The memory of past – an empty plate.

Ponder upon your cursed, shallow soul
The choice you've made when choosing was allowed
Domesticate the creature, break the mould
To hide your treachery and cheat the crowd.

The void forgave it in its savage wrath
Time turned itself in measurable fear
From infinite prevailing its jinxed path
For king or poor – the end is always near.

IT'S YOUR TURN TO SAY SORRY, PUTIN!

By Loraine Saacks

It's time to come clean now Putin –
Your pal, Bashar did use Sarin.
Your dastardly deeds – classified as *'Putiny'* –
Will shortly subject you to severe scrutiny –
Confession time's dangerously near,
Show you're sorry now, Vladimir.

Apologies aren't your forte, Vladimir,
Dismissing death tolls with your air, cavalier,
You think you're a Czar, presiding through
fear,
Venal villainous, vain Vladimir.

The Third Reich were hell-bent on extermination,
Willy Brandt lamented, with stark realization,
Apartheid would not work, grasped F W de Klerk,
And Australia also faced shame;
For established abuse, there was no excuse,
Aborigines heard Kevin Rudd claim.

Be mindful: some years before toxic bombs,
And after Czar Alex showcased the Pogroms,
Nick Romanov, his son, autocratic and mean,
Saw his power fade fast, with his friend, Rasputin.
Anti-migrant, arrogant, intransigent Vladimir
You'd better repent or you might disappear.

A Thought

By Nina Yakimiuk

When death encloses the mirage of life
It is as if night steals over the joy of day.
But, however brief the time
It is the bliss of day that
Makes the restful darkness worthwhile

ANTI – SOCIAL

By Samantha Edwards

I'm not alone, can't you see,
I got my phone right here with me.
where ever I go - in case of emergency.

I don't leave home without it
What if, you can't get hold of me.
That's traumatic,
That's disaster,
Major travesty.

No noti-fi-cations...pinging
Around my ears to gently lead
Into a con-ver-sation,
Motivated virtually

Got no time to meet old friends
For coffee, lunch or tea.
Just slide up, in my DM's connecting's so easy.

It's a slight addiction
Chatting on the go...
There's no need to look around
Cos everyone you know,

Is looking down with up turned palms
Devices staring back.
Missing seconds, minutes, hours
Life is so off track

But you can't say, that you want change
When u don't - hear ot- hers talk-ing
Cos everyone's so self-absorbed
While in this world we're wal-king

Live streaming... no longer dreaming
Of a better day ahead.
I think, life's screaming

And all our dreaming
Is buried doubly dead.

With just a gentle touch of hand,
We drift along distracted.
Forget the day of drudgery,
I'll follow - she's now added.

It’s hard to know what's really real
While living 'socially'
It’s time to stop, look, listen
Put the phone down,
Then you'll see.

The possibilities are all around
No more life pre-ten-ding.
And say hello with mouth and hand,
No text or pictures trending.

So I'll pick up my phone today,
Whilst thinking carefully.
Casually smile at strangers
While present in society.

I guess it’s the beginning
Of truly living socially
Let’s try for the beginning
Of truly living socially

The Old Pianist

By Ana Castellani

How are his hands still fast enough
Or his memories, how do they all combine
To create the loveliest of sounds
Even in his very old age?
His black velvet suit, with round golden buttons
His hand, their long fingers caressing the keys,
Blue eyes, the kind of blue only grandpas' have -
Through which they see the world...
A different world. Not this. Not here. Not me.

SOME GALLIC FANCY

By Loraine Saacks

Where's the Nicholas Winton of this gruesome era?
The stalwart defender of children from terror?
Will you go knocking on every front door?
To ask if they'll dish up some food for one more?

Does your heart not sink as these minors are thrown,
From a violent past to a future unknown?
Could you gun children down or bomb their existence –
The naïve, innocent, those with no resistance?

And yet they arrive,
Though barely alive,
In a foreign camp zone,
Confused, all alone,
Condemned just to roam,
With nowhere to call home.

Does a young child know why his family all fled?
And why, now he's here, both his parents are dead?
Is he able to sum up why he's lost in Calais;
Exhausted, abandoned, destitute – easy prey?

So, who's motivated to surf old archives?
Who'll stand guarantee that each child survives?
Lord Dubs has vowed he'll reciprocate,
For the last Kinder Transport which altered his fate?

Don't submit these children to some Gallic fancy,
If you turn away, they'll end up in a Drancy.

Tell Your Story

By Edna Herbert

Tell your story
How they came and pursued
Tell your story
Without being rude.
Tell your story
To educate the masses.

Tell your story
About the sound clashes.
Tell your story
Called the community theme.
And side by side
We loved as a team.

Tell your story
About the water fights,
And after raving
We'd walk home during the night.
Tell your story
About chicken rice and peas on a Sunday,
That tastes even better on a Monday.

Tell your story
Of the flowered enamel plates
With the blue rim.
Tell your story
About going to the barbers for a trim.

Tell your story
Saturdays watching
Tiswas on the telly.
And giant Haystacks
With his big fat belly.
Tell your story
About the grip
And as children
"You dare not go in it."

Tell your story
From your points of view.
I remember
That was on the telly too.

Songs That Remind Me of You

By Cleo Felstead

Songs that remind me of you.
In my heart and through my senses
The hand that always receives mine,
Night into day
Always ready, always real.

Songs that remind me of you.
With your dancing limbs and all the fun of the fair
The memories that live within
Belly laughs and knowing glances
Your hand against my cheek in the birthing room.

Songs that remind me of you.
The movement of your character through the seasons
Seeing myself reflected in you
To share our bed, to talk of the times before,
To live in mutual content amongst each other.

Songs that remind me of you.
Silently observing ourselves together in peace
The breath of our son
Simply knowing you will be home soon
The space between us and the bridges that join.

Songs that remind me of you,
Looking at each other,
Listening and saying yes.

These are the songs that remind me of you.

PRISONER OF TIME

By Ana Castellani

I see your hollow shape in my now empty bed
A thousand empty nights I'd trade for your return
I would ignore my time and have your life instead
I'd choose another name, in your world I'd adjourn.

I'm floating from the skies and step into your room
Just like I used to do so many nights before
I tread on shattered glass, my steps befall your doom
I ceased to be a star for the man I adore.

I sense the coldness of my tears and their caress
I broke from my eternal cage to follow you
My world is shuddering, I'm cursed with loneliness
I see, I hurt, I feel - your dream of me comes true.

White satin sheets, cover my sacrilege in blood
My ransom reminds me of what I've left behind
My former dreams are locked inside a blossom bud
A short but happy life to live amongst your kind.

DITCHING THE CZAR

By Loraine Saacks

Though I see you each morn, I don't know you at all;
I peer deep in your eyes,
Trying to analyse,
As I walk down my hall, and you gaze from my wall.

I don't need recall, to know you were tall,
Your five sons inherited height,
And I think you're exquisite, a pin-up exhibit –
You'll always be my lodestar light.

Your eyes would have flashed,
As you dared – and you dashed –
I don't blame you for ditching the Czar –
Who wants conscription for twenty-five years?
To Siberia, where memory of home disappears,
And it's rare to return from so far?

I'd have wept if I'd watched from that Pale of Despair,
If my son had to flee, to find safety – somewhere.
But, how *did* you go,
Is what I want to know;
Did you lay low in sweat, then, in heavy disguise,
Make your move at midnight, dodging the mogul's spies?

From your photo, I see, you're not short of a finger –
If you'd cut one off, they'd have let you malinger
Instead of starving and stumbling through snow,
Escaping the call-up, bypassing Moscow.

Now, you're framed – hung in state – half way up the wall,
And when I behold you, I'm always in thrall,
If you hadn't escaped, I'd not be here at all,
Is what you're telling me, strung up high in my hall.

One Plain, One Pearl

By Siobhan Reardon

You knitted me a jumper. With a hat to match.

It was a colour somewhere between moonstone and the shade of the mountains at the back of your house.

You measured me tenderly while I obediently stood, and lifted my arms up.

I was the problem child, who came to you in the days of summer. Who spoke little and ate less, full of feeling, obstinately wordless. While your own children, free as the wind, laughing and loud, elbowed their way to the table and dropped into the ocean directly.

I was too scared of all your happiness but I couldn't say that.

So you knitted for me what you wanted to say – you knitted me rock and wind and sea, you knitted me that I am where I belong, that I am loved, that I am me. You knitted me my heart, my young girl's privacy.

Years later, your strong sons carried you on their shoulders, as you always knew they would. And I came back across the ocean, the sea laid out below me, rustling, blue grey with grief.

And I walk in many places now. In suburban streets. In the city in the dazzle of the day. In hills and dips and, continents and sun-glazed walkways, and places where I do not belong, and do not want to.

I know now the joy of jumping in the ocean. Of the hand held, the smile beckoning, the dancing and caressing, the loneliness and lust of living.

But I am that girl. One plain, one pearl. And wherever I walk - your silent promise, an old blue hat in my pocket around which my fingers gently curl.

HAIKU; YOU

By Samantha Edwards

In the sun we smiled
Familiar the feeling
My heart leaped within

Sounds of laughter. High.
Reminds me that love lives here.
I know you well. JOY.

The dark cloud rolled in.
Thunder, lightning, only rain.
Your smile no more. Why?

Tears where the sun shone.
Summer erased before time.
Your smiles live in me.

SECTION II: STORIES

THE GREY LAKE

Trish Gomez

Leaning heavily on his walking cane, John Walsh limped to the drawing room window and stared out at the colourless garden. He turned to look over his shoulder at Captain Charles Beresford standing by the fire. "I saw her. You know she was by the lake."

Charles looked up from his contemplation of the flames and removed one highly polished boot from the brass fender, a sudden frown marring his handsome features.

John tried not to resent his friend's vigorous frame and regimental success. At thirty-four, the captain cut a particularly fine figure in scarlet regimentals. Cheated of his own expectations by an injury that saw him invalided out of the army, John turned his back on his friend, not wanting him to glimpse the bitterness he nursed. The sight of a pallid November sun through the window did little to lift either his spirits or the dismal landscape beyond the garden, where a bare field dotted with skeletal trees led down to a grey, shimmering body of water edged by a willow copse. For a moment, he thought he saw Emma again, standing at the lakeside. He closed his eyes, and whispered, "she's not a figment of my imagination," but there was no sign of her when he re-opened them. A stray tear rolled down his cheek which he dashed away with the back of his hand.

Charles patted his shoulder, making him jump. He hadn't heard him cross the room. "You know it can't have been her, don't you?" Charles' tone was unnaturally quiet.

He shook his head. "But I did see her, as clearly as I see you!"

"Maybe you did see Emma," Charles said with a shrug. "I understand, I really do. Now come back to the fire." He tried to steer John away from the window.

"But you don't," John protested. "You think Emma's death has unhinged me." He twisted free of Charles' unwanted shepherding grasp and hobbled across to the sideboard. Taking the stopper from a crystal decanter, he poured a generous measure of brandy into a glass and glowered at Charles. "I suppose you'd like one?" There was a note of peevishness in his voice. "Or should I ask Mrs Hodges to make you a nice cup of tea?" Charles' passive manner seemed to fuel his anger, which was irrational as the man had only ever tried to help. But nothing about the situation was rational.

"Now look here, John. I've never said, or come to that thought, anything of the kind," Charles protested. "And yes, I'll have that brandy."

The crack in Charles' composure lifted John's mood. "That's good because Mrs Hodges goes to her sister's on Wednesdays and won't be back until the morning."

They took their drinks over to the fire and sunk down into the worn leather armchairs. John reflected on their friendship as he sipped his drink. He'd always considered Charles more brother than friend, so of course it was ridiculous to think Charles would condemn him as mad.

*

The Hansom cab halted at the corner of King Street and St James Square where Captain Beresford alighted. The hall porter held the military club door open. The captain stopped in the lobby to have a word with the man. The porter assured him the major was in the building, and directed him to the first floor. Charles found his friend reclined in a comfy chair, by one of the large windows overlooking a quadrangle. His head resting against a chair-wing, eyes closed, gentle snores escaped a half-open mouth, peppering the silence. A partly read broadsheet rested on his knees and an empty glass sat on a small table at his elbow.

Charles cleared his throat. "Sir... Major McCallum... sir?"

Douglas McCallum's lids fluttered open and his unfocused blue orbs stared at him. "Good God!" He sprang to his feet, the paper forgotten. "Beresford," he thrust out a hand. "You're a rare sight in the club these days." He waved at the vacant chair on the opposite side of the window. "Sit, sit..."

Settling in the armchair, Charles said, "I must apologize for disturbing you here, sir but I'm concerned about the health of a mutual acquaintance." Pausing on sighting a waiter, he signaled to the man.

Douglas accepted a 'wee dram' in his lyrical Scots brogue.

"Do you remember John Walsh?"

"Wasn't he your young lieutenant in Corfu, you brought him into the infirmary? Got his leg mangled in an accident with an ammunition cart. He owes you his life."

"I think that's an overstatement but yes, he's the man. I'd say it was your handiwork that saved him."

"Good thing you got him there when you did. If it had been left any longer he'd have lost his leg and possibly his life too."

The waiter arrived with their drinks putting a momentary halt to the conversation.

"Your health," Douglas saluted with his glass before savouring its contents. "So, it's Walsh is it? Problem with his leg?"

"Not exactly," Charles hedged. "It's not quite that simple. The problem has more to do with his state of mind." He paused, took a sip from his glass then announced. "John thinks he's seen a ghost."

Douglas's eyes widened. "Good God. What in heaven's name made him think that?"

"It's tragic, really. Did you know he married shortly after leaving the army?"

Douglas shook his head.

"Well, Emma, that was his wife, drowned about a month back in the lake near Beachwood House. Naturally John is devastated but he's become obsessed with the idea he's seen her since, walking by the lake."

"Ah, silly question, but are you absolutely sure she's dead?"

"I walk with John when I can, and I was with him that day. He saw something in the water. I didn't realise at first it was Emma. John recognised her grey gown. In truth, I was the one who ran into the lake and wrestled her body onto the shore, too late to save her life. If John had been on his own, I doubt he'd have had the strength to pull her out the water."

"So she's the ghost . . ." Douglas queried, as he fumbled to straighten the newspaper.

Charles nodded. He picked up the water jug and added a dash more to his glass. "They met while John was convalescing. She lived with her aunt and uncle after her parents' death. Her uncle was the parish parson and the aunt a committed village worthy, which the niece was encouraged to emulate."

Douglas nodded. "I take it her death was an accident?"

Charles shrugged. "That's the coroner's verdict. Most likely theory is she saw something in the water, a dog in difficulties or bird maybe, and went in after it. Seems she had a weakness for animals in distress. But . . ."

"But you have your doubts?" Douglas guessed, giving up on his efforts to straighten the newspaper.

"If I'm honest, I'm not sure." Charles hesitated before placing his glass on the table. "Once she'd waded in, it'd be easy enough for her gown to snag on something hidden under the surface. Or maybe she just tripped. Her clothes would soak up the water like a sponge. The weight would make it difficult to stand. I don't think she could swim."

"But even so, you don't believe it was an accident, do you? Have you a reason for thinking she'd take her own life? Or is it something more than that?"

Charles shook his head. "As I said, I'm not sure. They married in haste and maybe the marriage didn't live up to either's expectations."

"Aye," Douglas nodded thoughtfully. He pulled a fob watch from his pocket. "Where are you staying tonight?"

"I've arranged for a room here."

"Good, can we continue this over supper?" He apologised, "only I've a consultation and need to prepare."

"Of course," Charles agreed. He was confident that once the major knew the extent of John's melancholia he would feel duty bound to offer his assistance.

*

Dressed against the early morning chill in a multi-caped greatcoat, John Walsh planted a low-crown top hat on his head and pulled his leather gloves on before sliding the bolts back on the front door. Leaning on the bulldog head cane, he limped down the steps and set off towards the lake. The trees creaked in the gentle breeze, like old men's limbs and underfoot leaves oozed their musky autumn aromas. A low-level mist covered the lake and made it impossible to tell where shore ended and the water began.

His injured leg, cramped with pain in the biting cold, making progress slow over the leaf-littered path. The closer he got to the lake, the more his senses were seduced by the gentle sound of lapping water and clean air. He could taste it on the damp breeze. Shivering, he remembered Emma floating face down in the murk.

A robin's song diverted his eye to the churchyard, where the bird sat on a bare branch, its head twisting to and fro as it watched him. He crossed the path and entered the church ground by the lychgate. Gravestones and moss-covered seraphs littered the graveyard. He followed the gravel path to the Norman church, standing a little apart from the rectory cottage where Emma had lived until her uncle's death shortly before they married. Now the place stood empty. John stopped in front of the vicarage staring at its blank windows, imagining Emma's face smiling down at him. The fresh earth of her grave stood out like a new wound, just off the path. No gravestone, the earth needing time to settle. The robin had followed him and sat on a weathered stone angel, chirping. It swooped down onto the grave and plucked a fat worm from the soil. The little bird's antics lifted his spirits, and for a moment, blocked the chilling image of Emma's death from his mind.

John glanced back at the cottage, and had the uneasy feeling of being watched, but saw no one. He didn't know whether to be relieved or upset that Emma hadn't reappeared. Hobbling now, he made his way to the gate and slowly retraced his steps towards Beachwood House. Startled by the raucous cry of a flock of rooks taking to the air he glanced over his shoulder and stopped dead as a woman in grey walked through the lychgate. She moved to the water's edge and stared across the lake, mist masking the hem of her gown. He couldn't tell whether she stood in the water or on the shore.

"Emma!" he cried in alarm as she appeared to wade into the lake. He tried to run, but the pain and weakness in his injured limb sent him sprawling. By the time he'd righted himself, she had disappeared. He swore, and scanned the shore and copse where a flash of grey moved amongst the willows. With the aid of his cane, he reached the scrubby woodland but now there was no sign of the woman. Frustration and disappointment overwhelmed him. He lashed out at the thicket with the cane. If only Charles had been with him, then he'd see she wasn't in his head.

*

Charles was first to arrive in the club's plush dining room. Seated at a secluded table behind an ornate column near a window he studied the décor. Mirrored walls reflected the light from elegant lamps and chandeliers that gave the room a golden glow. Through the window, the flickering mellow glow of gas street lamps pierced the black night. Men in formal attire occupied a number of the other tables.

Major McCallum appeared a few minutes later and apologised for his tardiness. After perusing the menu and consulting the maître d', both men decided on fillet of beef accompanied by a selection of seasonal vegetables. The major ordered a bottle of wine to accompany their meal.

While waiting for the first course, they caught up on the gossip of past and present friends in the regiment. Charles was surprised at how hungry he felt when the soup arrived, and tucked into his dish of tangy ham and pea broth.

Conversation was sparse as they ate. Heaving a satisfied sigh, Douglas dabbed a linen napkin to his salt and pepper flecked moustache. "Aye, they know how to make a good broth, I'll give them that." He relaxed into his chair and glanced at Charles. "You were saying earlier you had doubts about Emma's drowning being an accident. What do you think happened?"

Charles toyed with his napkin. "Well, as I mentioned, they didn't waste any time in getting married. I think they both had their reasons; John was feeling quite melancholy at living on his own. The pain in his leg doesn't help. It restricts him getting around. And from what he's said, Emma's aunt kept her on a close rein. Not surprising she would want her own establishment, but she never really settled into the role of wife." He smiled, recollecting his friend's complaints; *she flits from place to place like a butterfly, never settles.* "John wanted his home run as a military establishment and Emma didn't grasp this, which put them at odds. John got angry if anything was out of place."

"Was there ever any violence towards the girl, do you know?"

"Not that I'm aware," Charles said. "I never saw any evidence."

"Good, good. I wouldn't want to think of Walsh ill-treating his wife."

Charles marshalled his thoughts while the waiters cleared their dishes and served the main course. Digging into his fillet of beef, he said, "Emma spent less and less time in John's company, preferring to walk, no matter the weather. This of course only exasperated John. I suggested she might enjoy a London season. I thought it would get John away from his obsession with order in the house."

"Did they go?"

"No, John saw danger in giving her freedom to jaunt around town. He doubted his ability to keep up with her, with reason. A small legacy from her parents meant she had plenty of pin money. And it's unlikely her social calendar would have remained empty for long. He'd be hard pressed to gavotte round a dance floor and wouldn't like being side-lined."

"Aye, that's true."

"I've suggested consulting a local doctor." Charles said, putting his cutlery together. He fancied a slice of pie and looked for the waiter. "But the village doctor is a doddery old thing. John wouldn't go anywhere near him. I also proposed a chat with the new parson again; he made it plain he wanted nothing to do with him. The parson's a young chap with a gaggle of children. The parsonage is too small for his brood, so they live in the village."

"Where's the aunt?"

"She also has a place in the village."

Douglas McCallum stared thoughtfully at the ornate lamp on the table. "Has anyone besides Walsh seen this apparition?"

"No," Charles said. "That's why I hoped you'd visit Beachwood House. Speak to him, see what you make of it all. I've promised I'll walk with him when I get back, but so far he's the only one to set eyes on this vision in grey." He picked up his wine glass and studied the contents. "I'm sure he's heading for an asylum or worse, if nothing is done to help him." He looked directly at the major. "Maybe you could prescribe a draught, or something. He's on edge all the time and drinking heavily. I'm sure, though he'd never admit it, that he blames himself for her death."

"I've little practice with problems of the mind." The major laughed. "Now give me a limb to hack off..."

"Nevertheless, I'd say you're John's best bet at gaining some sort of peace of mind."

"I suppose I could come down next week."

"Capital!" Charles enthused, his goal achieved.

*

Major McCallum was as good as his word, arriving at Charles' lodgings on the Tuesday evening. They breakfasted early the following morning and made their way to Beachwood House. Mrs Hodges opened the door to them and as they shed their topcoats. "He's still in his bed." She tutted. "Another night's heavy drinking, I wouldn't wonder."

"I'll go and rouse him," Charles offered, taking the stairs two at a time. He found John half-dressed, sprawled across the bed on his back, snoring. He strode across to the windows and threw back the drapes, drenching the room in the harsh morning light.

John stirred and flung an arm across his eyes. "Close the damned curtains."

"For goodness" sake man you've got to put a stop to this." Charles crossed the room and stared down at his dishevelled friend.

"I saw her, you should have been there." He protested, easing himself up on to an elbow. "God, my head hurts! I swear there's an army marching through it." He blinked at Charles. "Please be a good fellow and pull the drapes."

"Major McCallum's waiting for you in the drawing room." Charles settled into a rattan armchair by the window. "You might want to tidy yourself up."

"In god's name why would I want to see him?" He fell back against the pillow. "I need something for my head. Ask Mrs Hodges for one of her magic powders, will you?"

"Only if you'll come and make yourself agreeable." Charles got up. "He's made a special effort to see you." He stopped by the door. "And do something about your attire."

"She was by the lake!" John shouted at Charles as he left the room.

By the time John arrived in the drawing room, Mrs Hodges had provided a tray laden with china and a coffee pot. She reminded them as she deposited her burden on the table that she'd be off to her sister's in a jiffy, and if they required anything further, they'd need to be quick.

Grinning, Charles watched her leave. "She used to scare the life out of me when I was a boy. I've always thought she'd make a fine Colour Sergeant."

Having put on a clean shirt and changed his trousers, John looked a little less crumpled, but his bloodshot eyes were heavy, and black stubble coated his jaw.

Both men stood as he entered. Charles said, "you remember Major Douglas McCallum." After a brief handshake, the major offered him coffee, which he waved away, going instead to the sideboard where he dispensed a measure of brandy. As an afterthought, he offered his visitors a drink, which was declined.

They settled into comfortable armchairs and Douglas enquired after John's health.

"No doubt Charles has been filling your ears with tales of hallucinations. Only they aren't you know. It's Emma I've seen by the lake."

"Aye, I was sorry to hear of your bereavement."

"Don't tell me; Charles wants your opinion on my sanity." He glared at the captain. "If you'd been here the other day, you'd have seen her too."

"No one's questioning your sanity, Walsh." The major said. "We're just concerned for your wellbeing. Tell me about Emma. What was she like?"

John topped up his drink and returned to the armchair. His eyes fixed on the glass, he told them about Emma. The words came slowly at first, then as if a dam had burst they tumbled out, he laid bare his frustration and resentment at having to leave the army and the disaster of his marriage. He choked on a sob and fell back onto the armchair, unable to stop the tears.

Unsettled, Charles kept his eyes averted, and busied himself with an imaginary speck on his sleeve.

Douglas placed a supportive hand on John's shoulder and squeezed, slipping him a clean pocket-handkerchief. "Give it time, and maybe a few days with a little less of this." He tapped the glass John clenched in his fist.

"This is my lifeline."

"Aye, but maybe there'd be a few less ghosts in both your waking hours and dreams without it." He scooped a handful of sachets from his medical bag. "These will be more effective and less harmful than brandy. But they're not to be taken with alcohol. Is that understood?"

"Yes."

The major dropped the packages on the sideboard and suggested a walk and a spot of lunch.

John excused himself with a weak grin. "Maybe tomorrow."

*

By the afternoon, Mrs. Hodges' magic powders had taken the edge off John's headache. Slumped in an armchair, he slept for a couple of hours and woke famished. The housekeeper had left a cold lunch in the pantry. John helped himself to a chunk of bread and topped it with sliced beef and pickles. He ate it in the kitchen being careful not to scatter Mrs. Hodges' scrubbed table-top with crumbs. He wanted to escape the silent, oppressive house. Opening the door onto the kitchen garden, he took a deep breath. The distant glint of grey water captured his attention. A walk to the lake may lift his black humour. And there was the hope he might see Emma.

He watched the sun sink below the horizon, disappointed at not seeing her. Turning his back on the last of the amber light and crossed the road to the lychgate. In the growing gloom he saw the robin perched on a gravestone, its pearl black eyes studying him. The bird appeared to be the same one he'd seen on previous visits. The way it flitted from place to place reminded him of Emma. A comforting thought struck him, and he smiled. Maybe the little fellow carried the souls of the dead up to heaven in its blood red breast.

The evening seemed endless in the quiet house. John stood in the library and ran an index finger across the spines of leather-bound books, looking for inspiration. He picked one and carried it back to the drawing room, reminding himself of his resolve to drink less. Settled in an armchair by the fire, he opened the volume and began to read. After just two pages he realised that not a word had sunk in. His vow to abstain from alcohol was ebbing, and he moved to the sideboard where he poured a cognac. Slumped back in his chair, he revisited the book. The cognac did little to improve his concentration and before long his head was nodding.

John woke with a start, and found the book had fallen to the floor. He spotted the sachets McCallum had left. Muttered, "why not," and emptied two sachets into a glass along with a shot of cognac. "Bottoms up," he said, and downed the contents.

He headed for the bedroom, seized the banister with one hand and holding a candlestick in the other, hauled himself up the stairs.

On entering the bedroom he collapsed on the bed where sleep instantly overtook him.

He woke in the early hours with a start, confused. A floorboard creaked on the landing, but it couldn't be Mrs Hodges going to bed - she was at her sister's.

He rolled onto to his side and stared into the darkness, his fuddled brain struggled to focus. The squeak of ungreased door hinges had John's heart thumping. Bit by bit the door opened, a light flickered and hovered for a moment, then inched towards the bed.

"Who's there?" he croaked, swallowing down bile. The rustle of silk and heady fragrance of lavender hit him. "Emma!" he breathed.

Her face, lit by the candle, appeared above him, forget-me-not blue eyes glowered down. He struggled to sit, but she placed a hand against his chest and pushed him back against the bed. He went to grab her, but she swatted his fists away like unwanted flies. "Am I dreaming, or are you a phantom?"

A feline smile brightened her eyes.

"I don't understand?"

"No you don't, do you? You really don't." She gave a burst of unholy laughter. "You never did understand me."

"I . . . I . . ."

"You never loved me, did you? You just wanted something to fill the void left by your discharge from the army. Someone you could order around, to bully."

"That's not true!" John tried to scoot up the bed. "It wasn't like that. I did," he faltered, "do, love you."

"No, you don't!" she shouted, droplets of saliva spattering his face. "You drove me into that lake. Your persistent carping . . . never satisfied. Army regulations, that's what you lived for." She placed the candleholder on the nightstand. "What about me, John? Did you ever consider my feelings? No, of course you didn't. That's why my life ended in the lake."

"No." He sobbed, "no."

She stood for a moment and stared at him, before unfastening the rope coiled about her slender waist.

"What's that for?"

She walked to the centre of the room, where she threw one end of the line over a solid timber ceiling beam. Dragging the rattan chair over to the rope, she hitched her skirts up and climbed on to the seat.

"Emma, what the hell are you doing? You mustn't end your life like this."

She smiled over her shoulder. "Oh, don't worry, it's not for me. Have you forgotten? I'm already dead."

He watched, dazed, as she secured the rope. Damn McCallum and his medication. The blasted stuff was making him hallucinate.

Emma hopped off the chair and stood back to admire her work. "What do you think?"

A noose, already formed in the rope, swayed back and forth above the chair. Its eerie shadow bounced around the bedroom walls.

"Now, my dear husband, it's time for you to join me in the afterlife." She came back to the bed and took hold of his hands.

"No!" he protested, struggling to free himself from her icy grip.

"But you must," she coaxed. "It serves no purpose for you to remain here. You must see how you're a burden to your friends. Mrs. Hodges considers you a waster, and tells this to the world. You'll be happy again once we're together. No more pain. It'll all disappear, my love."

"No . . . I don't know."

Emma yanked his hands, again. "Come on, you know it's right."

He put his feet to the floor and an army of smithies were suddenly at work in his head. He felt sick, and leaning on Emma, he staggered towards the swaying rope desperate for it to be an illusion. He collapsed into the rattan chair. "I'm going to pass out."

Emma searched the folds of her gown and produced a small bottle of smelling salts.

John jerked away as vinegar vapours assaulted his nostrils.

Emma bent over him and reached for the noose.

*

"He's still away in his bed." Mrs. Hodges said as she let Captain Beresford and Major McCallum in to the hall. "I've only just this minute returned from my sister's. There's no sign of Master John having been down for breakfast." She gestured towards the coat stand. "And his greatcoat and cane are still there, so he's not out walking"

"I'll go and rouse him." Charles offered, moving towards the staircase.

"You may well have a job. There's an empty decanter in the drawing room," the housekeeper informed him, her tone caustic.

Charles entered the darkened bedroom and pulled the heavy drapes open, letting pale morning light fill the room. Turning from the window, he flinched and uttered an oath before calling McCallum to join him.

Douglas recoiled at the appalling sight of Walsh's lifeless body swaying at the end of a rope.

"Suicide, God forgive him." Charles grunted.

"Would seem so," he replied. "Did he leave a note?"

"What?" Charles shook his head. "Oh, not that I've seen."

Douglas caught sight of something glinting on the floor and bent down to retrieve an open smelling salts bottle by the dressing-table leg. He turned it over in his hand, curious to know what it was doing there, and showed it to Charles.

"It's probably been there some time, dropped by Emma maybe and rolled out of sight. Just not been noticed," Charles offered.

"Maybe." Douglas placed the bottle on the nightstand next to a candle stub. He was surprised to see a second spent candle sitting beside it. "We'll need to inform the county magistrate," he said, scrutinizing the room again. There was a note of discord that he couldn't quite pin down. "There'll have to be a coroner's inquest."

"The coroner's jury are sure to find John's sanity affected by Emma's drowning, aren't they?" Charles looked at the major. "It doesn't bear contemplating that they'd judge his death a felony."

A sudden shiver ran down Douglas' back. He looked to the window, but it was closed. His mother would say; it's someone walking over your grave. Walsh's chilly footsteps, perhaps. The man must have been deeply distressed to take his own life. A pang of guilt made him consider if he could have done more to prevent this tragedy. He turned to Charles. "Time to send a message to the magistrate, I think."

*

Within twenty-four hours of the inquest verdict, Major McCallum and Captain Beresford stood by the lychgate awaiting the hearse's arrival. Witnessing a burial at ten on a stormy night was a prospect Douglas didn't relish. He turned the collar of his greatcoat up, against the icy blast sweeping across the lake and huddled into its warmth. Anxious for the safety of his top hat, he'd secured it in place with a long black woollen scarf.

"Is that the jingle of harness?" Charles asked raising his lantern to light the street. The screeching wind made it difficult to discern the sound. "Yes, I'm sure it is." He grunted, stamping his feet against the cold. "This is a God-awful time for a funeral."

"Better a funeral at night in consecrated ground than in a God forsaken ditch at some nameless crossroad with a stake pinning him to the grave, which would have been his fate a few years back," the major reminded him.

"True, very true," Charles nodded. "And I thank heaven the inquest saw fit to decree temporary insanity. But obviously the verdict isn't good enough for the parson." He glanced at the clergyman lurking under a tree. "He wouldn't hear of a day time funeral."

"And you'll not do too badly by that verdict." Douglas pointed out. "Walsh's assets won't go into the Government's coffers. So there'll be something for you to inherit."

"That is harsh, sir. I was devastated by John's tragic end and do not look to profit from his or his dear wife's death."

The hearse's arrival put an end to their conversation. Gleaming black horses pulled the ornate carriage with large glass windows. Clinging to his top hat, the funeral director greeted them. "Sirs, this is a sad affair." He said bowing. "But everything has been arranged as you would wish."

Pallbearers joined McCallum and Beresford to assist in carrying the unadorned coffin. Beachwood House had yielded one mourner, the elderly head gardener, who took his place in the line. Two men carried lanterns to light the way.

Stepping from the shadows, the parson opened his prayer book and clamped the fluttering pages with a hand while reading from the text. The handful of mourners, took little notice of the service. No sooner had the parson tossed a fistful of dirt onto the coffin lid than the mourners were on their heels, eager to get out of the gusting wind. No doubt heading for the warmth of their firesides, Douglas thought.

A gravedigger appeared from the gloom and planted a shovel in a waiting mound of earth. In no particular hurry, he surveyed the cavity. Leaning on the shovel, he said. "Who'd have thought the young lieutenant here would've gone and done such an ungodly thing. I reckons there's a curse on that god-awful place." He jerked his head towards Beachwood House.

"Please, excuse me for a moment," Charles said, stepping away from them. "I've to settle up with the parson." He shot McCallum an apologetic smile. "Only agreed to be here because I said I'd pay him under the counter, so to speak."

The gravedigger's watched Charles as he walked towards the loitering clergyman. "That one's fond of under the counter dealing."

"The parson?" Douglas queried, watching Charles delve into the pocket of his greatcoat to withdraw a healthy-looking purse.

"No sir, the captain."

"Oh really," Douglas gave him a sharp look. "You've had dealings with him before?"

Avoiding the major's eyes, the gravedigger made much of rolling up his shirtsleeves. "Beg pardon, I didn't mean to speak out of turn, sir."

"Aye, of course not," Douglas said, taking a few pennies from his pocket. "I'm just intrigued to know what my friend's been up to."

"I ain't no peacher," The man said, eyeing the coins Douglas jingled in his hand. "Mind you, it did seem mighty queer him wanting a young woman's corpse. Thought it best not to ask too many questions, knowing that some gentlemen have what you might call unnatural tastes, and all."

"You gave him a body!" Douglas dropped the coins.

Crouching, the gravedigger grabbed a lantern and held it over the spot where the money had fallen.

"You gave him a body!" Douglas repeated. "You know that breaks the law?"

"God love you, sir. I ain't no resurrection man, not me sir. I'm more your intermediary, sir," he reassured McCallum as he unearthed the coins and pocketed them. "I knows the man, that knows the man, if you get my drift, sir."

Charles had finished his transaction and was on his way back to them.

Under his breath and eyeing Charles, Douglas asserted. "Aye, that's as maybe but I advise you not to breathe a word of this to anyone. You understand?"

"Right you are, sir." The gravedigger tapped the side of his nose. "Now I best be getting on with planting the gentleman before this little breeze sweeps us all into the lake."

*

"Major Douglas McCallum?" The magistrate asked, stretching out a hand of welcome. "I understand you've something of importance to tell me."

Settling back in a brown leather armchair the magistrate indicated, Douglas felt his gut clench. He didn't want to put his suspicions into words. "It's difficult to know where to start," he hesitated, "maybe Corfu. Lieutenant John Walsh had the misfortune to injure his leg while stationed there. That's when I first met him. But it was some eighteen months later when Captain Charles Beresford called on me at my club and asked for my help. He was troubled by Walsh's behaviour after his wife's death."

Douglas cleared his throat and chronicled the events leading to Walsh's apparent suicide. He paused to sip from a glass of water, and looked at the magistrate. "Well, sir, after the yarn spun by the gravedigger, I decided to do some investigating of my own. My doubts were initially aroused when Beresford found Walsh's body. Something was off; the additional candle on the nightstand, smelling salts bottle on the floor. Mrs Hodges struck me as a diligent housekeeper and would never allow such tardiness."

"You didn't believe he'd had a visit from an apparition?" A flicker of amusement lit the magistrate's eyes. "And who's ever heard of a ghost needing a candle to light their way."

"Aye, well that's as maybe, but in all honesty, I thought the wee ghostly woman in grey was in Walsh's head, just as Beresford had intended. But knowing Beresford had acquired a woman's corpse put a different complexion on things. Maybe it wasn't Emma, but a substitute pulled from the lake. Walsh was in shock and I doubt he saw her properly. The grey gown enough to convince him he'd seen his wife. Beresford, by his own admission, took charge of the situation."

"Then Lieutenant Walsh may well have seen his wife after her supposed death," the magistrate surmised. "And what of Mrs Walsh? Where is she now? If your conjecture is correct she must also be part of the plot."

"Aye, her aunt confirmed she was disenchanted with the marriage, which tallies with Beresford's account, but he neglected to mention that he'd been encouraging Emma in her grievances. The aunt didn't approve of the Captain. She considered the bonds of marriage as sacred; Emma had made her bed and now must lie down in it."

The magistrate gave a considered nod. "Assuming the woman's alive; is there a place she could stay without being seen?"

"Well there's the wee parsonage," Douglas suggested. "It's empty now. Too small for the new parson and his brood." He leaned forward. "It would make an ideal base; secluded, direct access to the churchyard and lake. Perfect if you don't want nosey villagers to see you. The upper windows have a good view of the path leading to Beachwood House."

"Have you investigated this possibility?"

"Aye, but I've no key, so I can only view the outside, and the place looks empty."

"Best leave it with me then," the magistrate advised. "Do you think Beresford's absconded with the woman?"

"Unlikely. Walsh used to joke when he was in hospital that I had to keep him alive because he didn't want Beresford becoming a wealthy man just yet. Seems he's left his estate to him. He had no close relatives. When they were in Corfu, Beresford used to brag Walsh was as good as a brother. I seem to recall someone telling me Walsh's father brought Beresford his army commission."

"You surprise me. I would have thought the Will would have been changed in favour of his wife."

Douglas shrugged, "Walsh hero-worshipped Charles, even more so after his accident."

"You were the army surgeon who operated on him in Corfu?"

"Aye, that I was," Douglas nodded.

"Well thank you for your candour," the magistrate said, rising to show him to the door. He assured him that he would investigate the matter. With his suspicions now under review by what Douglas considered the appropriate authorities, he returned to his London lodgings to complete his plans for departure to the garrison in Corfu.

*

Several months after his return to Corfu, Douglas' eye was caught by the headline in a copy of the *London Morning Post*. On finding a comfortable chair in a quiet corner of the officers' mess, he unfolded the newspaper. The sensational header: *Wife's Ghost Complicit in Husband's Suicide* titled a report from an Old Bailey murder trial. Douglas scanned the article, which confirmed Captain Charles Beresford's part in his friend's death. His relief at the verdict was tinged with the discomfort of not having recognised Beresford's evil intent in time to save Walsh.

Emma, discovered hiding in one of the parsonage's closets, had turned on her partner in crime, following the disclosures in her aunt's and the gravedigger's statements. Pleading Queen's Evidence and insisting the handsome captain had beguiled her, she revealed the full extent of the felony and ensured Beresford had a date with the hangman's noose. It troubled Douglas that Beresford had saved his friend's life only to kill him a few months later. He speculated on how big a part Emma had played in the scheme, and prayed her spell in jail would be a long one. The arrival of an orderly ended the major's reflection. He folded the newspaper and left it for others to read.

LOVE POTION

Robert Williams

My name is Margaret, although most people call me Mags, and I am an urban witch.

There, that's the difficult part out of the way. I try not to beat about the bush when it comes to my job. I'm a witch who lives in a tower block in an unfashionable part of London. There are a few of us about but we try to keep it low key. You wouldn't be able to tell that I was a witch by looking at me. In fact, many people think I'm a librarian or even a nurse. Both are sort of true. Modern witchcraft is a vocation that requires many skills.

People come to me with problems, problems they can't take to anyone else, and I do what I can for them. Most of the time, they just need sympathy and a cup of tea or a nudge in the right direction. Sometimes they need a little bit more.

I hadn't decided what Bruce and Jenny needed yet. A kind word, perhaps, or maybe Relate's phone number or the address of the swingers' club around the corner. Time would tell.

Bruce looked like a moderately successful used-car salesman, all sharp suit, shaved head and bright shiny eyes that darted around the room as if looking for what he could sell. He had dressed carefully and well. Nothing he wore was cheap, but he had stopped short of flashy. He let himself down, however, by looking me in the eye too often and using my name every other sentence. He spoke in that earnest tone that politicians use when they are lying. Or just talking. You know politicians.

"Mags, this is a lovely cup of tea."

"Thanks. It's just Sainsbury's. Nothing special."

"It really hits the spot. You sure you've not put anything extra in it?" He laughed in that way people do when they think they've said something funny and they want you to know. Or maybe he was nervous.

"I'd charge you more if I had."

Jenny looked like a trophy bride, a gorgeous woman who was far out of Bruce's league. I guessed he had married her to look good on his arm. Goodness knew how she had been persuaded to marry him.

He seemed, however, to have no interest in her as a person. His body language – witches are fluent in body language – ignored her completely but his indifference didn't matter to her. She just smiled. She smiled a lot, but the smile looked genuine. She looked pleased. Pleased to be with him, pleased with who she was and pleased to be here. That last one had me foxed. Her designer clothes and handbag looked so out of place in my kitchen that I found myself trying to hide the hole in my second-best cardy whenever she looked in my direction.

"More tea, Jenny?"

"Thank you, yes. That would be delightful." Her accent was odd and that was one more thing that intrigued me about the couple. It wasn't right. It sounded very landed gentry and enormously fake. It would have been ideal for a TV costume drama. Her accent was exactly like Lady Mary's from *Downton Abbey,* but it didn't suit her.

"Another biscuit?"

"Oh no. I couldn't. I've got to watch my figure." She glanced at Bruce with a knowing smile. He preferred her slim, or so she thought. I could see he really couldn't give a toss.

I talked about my services but kept to topics I knew they wouldn't want such as finding missing cats and curing gout. I really just wanted to watch them some more. People let down their guard when they are listening, and they think no-one is watching.

Bruce, I could see, was waiting for an opportunity to speak. His eyes darted furiously as his brain tried to frame questions that he could ask. I could see him become frustrated as I fed him enough to have something to ask me only to supply the answer a few seconds later. It didn't matter. He had other questions to ask. That much was obvious.

As I spoke, Jenny smiled in an apparently distracted way, yet she was listening intently. Her eyes never left me the whole time I was speaking, not even when she blinked.

"Are you okay there, Jenny?" I used the opportunity to lean in closer to her and take a good look in her eyes. The eyes aren't, as any good witch will tell you, the windows to the soul, but they are an infallible indicator of someone's state of mind.

This wasn't a case of Jenny's smile not reaching her eye. Jenny's ever-present smile did reach her eyes and she was genuinely happy. She believed it with almost every ounce of her being.

"Of course." She smiled at Bruce, who looked away. "Everything is absolutely fine"

The key word to remember was ‘almost’. She believed in her own happiness with *almost* every ounce of her being. Almost. I could see in her eyes a tiny core of Jenny looking out, and it wasn’t happy. Inside, deep inside, she raged. I didn’t let on that I knew but I could see that she’d noticed. Her smile didn’t waver, but the rage intensified. I nodded to show that I would try to help her but, as to how, I didn’t have a clue.

“How can I help?” I asked, directing my question at Bruce.

His salesman-smile faded, and his eyes lost their twinkle. For the first time, I noticed the fine wrinkles around them and the dark shadows underneath. He was tired. Very tired.

“Well, it’s tricky,” he began.

“If it were easy then you wouldn’t be here.”

“You’re not wrong, Mags. You’re not wrong.” He looked into space, articulating his thoughts. Why was he hesitating? Had it anything to do with Jenny’s anger?

“Jenny and I have been married a long time,” he said.

“How long?”

“Three years.”

“Three years?” I was incredulous but tried not to show it.

“Three blissfully happy years,” Jenny said through her smile.

“Yeah, happy” Bruce added. I wasn’t convinced. Something wasn’t right here.

“Then, what’s the matter?”

Bruce looked at Jenny for the first time since they had arrived, and her face lit up. She looked like a dog that had been promised a walk, but his face showed nothing except weariness. He took a long look at me and his tiredness was palpable.

“Three years can feel like a lot longer, you know.”

I nodded. I think I knew where this was going.

“Every night. Every sodding night.”

“Sex?”

He nodded.

“We make love every night,” Jenny added. “Bruce is such a beast.”

He shook his head and then buried his face in his hands.

“Three hours every night. I can’t do it, Mags, I really can’t” he said. He was almost crying. “I just want to sleep.”

I patted him on the shoulder and he jumped. He looked up and relaxed when he saw it was me.

“You want me to calm her down?”

“Or give me something.”

“What?”

"I don't know. Energy. Stamina. Will-power. The ability to say no."

"Have you tried your GP?"

"He just laughed and said he wished he was so lucky."

"You can buy Viagra over the counter these days."

"I don't need it."

"Little Bruce is always ready to perform," Jenny said with a giggle.

"It's the rest of me that's knackered, Mags. My todger has a life of its own. Even though I'm ready to drop, it still springs up as soon as we're in bed."

That really didn't sound right. There was more to this than just nymphomania. I was beginning to suspect that something else was at work.

"Let me try something," I said and got up. "More tea?"

They both nodded so I put the kettle on to boil and went to look for my dowsing rod. My best theory was that Jenny and possibly Bruce as well were under the influence of love spells, but I needed to be certain.

The law doesn't recognise witchcraft, and, by extension, it doesn't do anything about craft-based crimes. To those in the know, however, a long-term love spell was a combination of rape and slavery. The Witch's Council had them banned in 1974. Not only was this sort of spell as close to illegal as you could get in the witching world but the witch who'd cast this one had truly messed it up. A love spell is basic stuff. A first-year trainee would have been able to mix a simple love potion from ingredients bought from Waitrose. There was virtually no scope for getting it wrong. Jenny should have loved Bruce body and soul and the angry spark I saw in her eyes shouldn't have existed.

I found my dowser, a Y-shaped willow branch, tucked away in my DIY cupboard. I knew I had left it in the kitchen, but willow has a habit of migrating. The dowser seemed to like my screwdrivers.

"The kettle has boiled," Jenny said, when I returned. "I did try to make the tea but I'm afraid I didn't know where you kept everything."

"Don't worry. I'll make some in a minute. Let's do this first."

I had them close their eyes and relax before I sat down. I held the rod loosely, one branch of the Y in each hand, my fingers finding familiar grooves and notches in the wood. I cleared my mind and concentrated on the roughness of the bark, the weight of the branch in my grasp and the way the rod seemed alive and about to dance on its own.

Then I spoke to it. Not out loud, of course. That sort of behaviour, talking to a stick, just makes the punters giggle. I just thought at it and I told it I wanted to find evidence of witchcraft, and immediately my arms were pulled by the rod, describing a circle and pointing at every part of my kitchen. My dowsing rod has a sense of humour. I told the rod to ignore anything of mine and immediately it pulled to my left. Jenny. A definite spell at work then.

Now, what about Bruce? I told the branch to ignore Jenny and it drifted slowly towards him. The reaction wasn't as strong as with Jenny. No, that wasn't right. The reaction was just as intense but there was another reaction that was pushing the rod away from Bruce. It was almost as if the dowsing rod feared him. That puzzled me, but I let it lie.

"Well, that's all in order," I said, putting the rod down. "Let's get that tea made."

I clattered about in the kitchen, making preparations.

"Why did you come to me?" I called out to them.

"I just told you," Bruce answered.

"No, why me, in particular. You don't look like locals."

Bruce laughed. "I used to live in this block on the twentieth."

"Ah. The penthouse flats." The top floor had been bought out in its entirety by property developers and converted from eighteen bog-standard flats into six "stunning luxury apartments" with their own dedicated express elevators. The apartments had been snapped up by pretentious idiots who didn't know the area very well and sold almost immediately for a third of their value when it emerged that the estate wasn't the best place to be parking cars that cost more than the average house.

"I loved that flat. I stayed there two years. I only moved when I married Jenny."

I was impressed.

"I even got to know some of the locals," he continued. "Everyone spoke highly of you, Mags. Everyone knows you."

"Here you are," I said with a flourish as I laid the tray on the table in front of them then poured each of them a cup.

"Thanks, Mags," Bruce said.

"Tell me about when you first met."

Bruce looked at Jenny and shrugged. He took a sip of the tea and grimaced before speaking.

"Back then, Jenny and I didn't really get on."

"Really?"

"I hated him," She said. The spark in her eyes still did.

"Mags, back then I wanted Jenny more than anyone, anything. I could think of nothing other than her and I vowed I would stop at nothing to get her."

"He kept at it. Persistence pays off," Jenny said.

"It came on gradually. As I kept pressing my case, she began to tolerate me, then accept me and then, finally, love me."

Ah, a cumulative spell. Probably a potion administered to her over a few months.

"How long did this take?"

"I don't know. Six months, I think."

"And how long has she been like this?"

We both glanced at Jenny who was looking at Bruce as if every word he'd said had been poetry.

"A couple of years."

"Does it ever change?"

"How do you mean?"

"Does she have off-days where she isn't so much of a puppy?"

"No, I don't think ..." he said slowly. "No, wait. Yes. She does. She gets a bit snappy with me every month. I thought it was ... you know."

I rolled my eyes. Men rarely get to grips with the concept of menstruation and few could talk about it easily. This wasn't the time to educate him, however.

I decided it was time to drop the bombshell.

"I think you are both under the control of love spells."

"What? How?" Bruce was shocked.

Outer-Jenny just smiled while inner-Jenny burned brighter.

I patted his hand and muttered reassuring words in his ear. He looked distracted for a few moments.

"Most likely, someone fed you a potion," I said, in a louder voice. "In Jenny's case, it was a sub-standard potion that wears off every month and has to be refreshed."

Jenny's eyes raged so brightly that I was surprised that Bruce didn't see it.

"Who on earth could be doing that to her?"

"I don't know but I intend to find out. Love spells are against the Witch's Code. Unless there was a good reason for this, the witch who did this is in big trouble."

I did the same thing with Jenny, patting her hand and muttering reassuring words in her ear. The rage in her eyes dimmed for a few seconds.

"Can you turn it off?" This was Bruce.

"Sort of."

"Sort of? What do you mean by that?"

"It's unorthodox but I could give you a love potion myself."

"You said that was illegal." I was glad Bruce had been paying attention.

"It's against the Witch's Code if there's no good reason. Not the same as illegal but close enough. This, however, is a good reason."

"How will it help?"

"My potion will overwrite the existing spell, but I will have control of it. I'll be able to modify its actions. Cancel it, for instance. What do you say?"

"We'll be normal?"

"Whatever that is for you, yes."

Bruce thought for a minute and then nodded his assent. I turned to Jenny.

"Will I still love Bruce?" she asked.

"You'll love him more. Better still, he'll love you with all his heart." Temporarily. That would end when I cancelled the spell. I didn't tell her that.

I suddenly doubted myself. Should I do this? I was planning on casting a spell that would eradicate Jenny's outer personality. I would be killing her. She was as innocent as a puppy and she would be gone when I had finished. Inner-Jenny would be back in control.

But that was as it should be. Outer-Jenny would have to die so that inner-Jenny, real-Jenny, could live.

I took in a deep breath, making up my mind, and then exhaled.

"Very well," I said. I couldn't let inner-Jenny continue to suffer. "I have already given you the potion."

They both jumped.

"I thought that tea tasted funny," Bruce said. "I don't feel any different though."

"You won't. This isn't the fourteenth century. Things have moved on as far as spells are concerned. I've primed you both with a code word. The potion won't take effect until you hear me say the right word. Are you ready?"

They both looked at me with a solemn intensity, daunted by what was about to happen. Jenny's eyes blazed. Almost in unison, Jenny and Bruce nodded.

"Look at each other, please." I didn't want them falling in love with me. I had the counter-spell ready, just in case. I didn't want to use it. My mum brought me up to not waste spells.

The words I had muttered in their ears earlier had primed them for the code word I was about to use.

"Marigold." My washing up gloves had been in view when I was speaking into Bruce's ear.

The effect was immediate. Bruce's eyes, which had previously looked at Jenny's left ear, locked onto her eyes, which in turn lost their red spark. Lustful grins split both of their faces and they lunged for each other.

"Sleep," I said, and the lunges ended gracelessly on my kitchen table. Love potions double quite nicely as sleeping potions given the right code word and I had primed them with more than one.

I made Bruce comfortable and then sat Jenny up in the chair. I needed to talk to her alone.

"Jenny! Jenny! Can you hear me?"

She groaned.

"Good. Listen to my voice, Jenny. Can you do that?"

"Bruce ..."

"He's right here, love. Don't worry. Now listen. I'm going to count down from three and click my fingers. At that point, the love potion will cease to work for you Jenny and you alone and you will wake up. You got that?"

She groaned again but nodded slowly.

"Three ... two ... one." Click.

"Jenny. You're back to your normal self. Tell me, who has been doing this to you? Was it Bruce? Has he been –"

"You stupid meddling witch!"

I have to admit that was not the response I was expecting.

"What?"

"You couldn't leave well enough alone, could you?" Her accent was now less *Downton Abbey* and more Deptford Market.

"What?" I know I repeated myself. I had no idea where the conversation was going.

"I administered the love potions, you idiot. Me! And they weren't substandard either."

"But why? You hate him. I could see that in your eyes."

"You saw me hating being dragged here. You saw me hating you poking your nose in where it wasn't wanted. You saw that!"

"No. That wasn't it."

"Yes, it was. Not only that. You are undoing years of work."

"What?" My vocabulary isn't the best when I am confused.

"Look at him."

I looked. Bruce was sleeping peacefully.

"What do you see?"

I saw Bruce, a man in his late thirties, asleep. His smooth head needed a shave, I suddenly noticed, and so did his face.

"A sleeping man."

"You're supposed to be a witch. Look properly."

His hair and his beard were growing noticeably, and I could see the gap between his eyebrows was narrowing.

"He's a werewolf?" I had encountered a few of those over the years but Bruce didn't fit. I could usually spot a werewolf a mile away, but Bruce wasn't one. Bruce was something else.

"No, a satyr."

"A satyr? And what are you? A nymph?"

She gave me a pitying look.

"I'm as human as you. I'm his Keeper."

Ah – that explained a lot.

"Bugger."

"Indeed. Thanks to you, we've got a sex-crazed time bomb ticking away in your kitchen."

"Sorry."

"I had him under control. My control. I fed him just enough potion to be interested in me and me alone every night and a much higher dose to myself to convince myself that I wanted him."

"But only enough so that you, the real you, were still able to watch him. That was why I could see that spark in your eye. The spell wasn't crap at all. It was meant to be like that. You had to watch. And so, you watched, and you hated. Don't say it was me you hated. I couldn't tell much from that spark, but I could see it was old."

She sighed, her anger against me spent. I had found the truth.

"Of course I hated him. I hated myself more. He found it exhausting fucking me. That was nothing compared to how I felt. Night after night making myself be used by that thing and the biggest part of me thinking I enjoyed it."

"But why do you do it?"

"Who else? Me or a member of my family has to wear him out or he'd be shagging most of London."

Keepers worked in families. Women and men allowed themselves to be used to keep all of the randy supernaturals from going crazy on all the poor humans. We owe them. We all owe them.

"It's all I've known since I had the kids. My family have been Keepers for generations. Satyrs, nymphs, werewolves, centaurs. We've kept them all. Our whole reason for existing is to keep things like him in check. My mother was a Keeper, and all my aunts. I took over on Bruce when my Aunt Sarah wanted to retire. Before her it was my Great Aunt Maureen and so on. Can you imagine the carnage if one of these things got loose in London?"

I stared at Bruce. "That has happened though, hasn't it?"

She sighed. "Well done. Yes. Jack the Ripper was a satyr. My many-times-great-grandmother got him under control eventually, but we lost three of her sisters along the way."

I continued to look at Bruce. His beard and hair had fully grown out. Horns had begun to poke out from his locks and his shoes had fallen off, exposing neat hooves.

"I could keep him asleep."

"He'll wake up. We've tried that with them in the past. We're just going to have to reinstate the spells I had in place."

"But you'll be trapped again. There has to be another way."

"There isn't. You're going to have to help me. We don't have much time."

"Wait! I have an idea."

She looked hopeful.

Half an hour later, Jenny led Bruce away, blind-folded. He went as meekly as a sedated satyr.

"Thanks, Mags, this is going to change my life. You have no idea."

"I think I have, Jenny. I'm glad I was able to help."

"Oh, here." She reached into Bruce's pocket and pulled out his wallet then thrust a large wad of money into my hand.

"That's too much."

"It's not enough, trust me."

I kissed her goodbye in answer and watched as she led him away. As they started walking down the stairs, I raised my hand to wave and realised I was still holding my mirror.

The thing about love potions is that the person under the spell falls in love immediately with the first person they see. When I activated the second potion, Bruce was staring at his own reflection.

I laughed as I shut the door behind me. She was going to have a terrible job of getting him out of the bathroom.

THE UN-BEAUTIFUL GAME

Ian D. Brown

The ramshackle stadium sits at the base of a natural bowl formed by the surrounding hillside, the uneven pitch threadbare and sandwiched at both ends between two old stands that have long seen better days. The vast openness that runs either side of the playing area is an open invitation for the wind to ride the banks and sweep straight through us, and it duly obliges.

It's been raining all day and is still bucketing down through heavy cloud cover as the referee raises the whistle to his lips and, with one long extended blow, brings the First Half to an end. We're three nil down away from home at half-time, and I've missed a penalty. I never miss penalties. I stepped up, planted my left foot next to the right-hand side of the ball and brought my right leg behind it in one swiveling motion. The Goalkeeper went the wrong way as planned. I'd done it a hundred times in training and scored every one, but this time the ball didn't follow the script, and floated in slow motion through the air against the post and trickled out of play. The last penalty I missed was about twenty years ago in my Mum's front room against my little brother when the ball clipped the leg of the coffee table and smashed her favourite vase.

I never like playing away matches up North; my top, shorts and socks are soaked through to the skin as we trudge off, and I can feel the rain battering us further into submission, ice cold and stinging my bare face and legs. Catapulted on the back of that swirling wind it feels like it's coming straight from the arctic itself.

As we head towards the far end of the ground the wall of noise generated from the home fans is deafening, they're massive underdogs and never in their wildest dreams had they expected to be in a position like this. They've whipped themselves up into the mother of all frenzies. For the sake of self-preservation I should keep my head down, but for some unknown reason as I approach the last row of seats behind the corner flag I turn my head to the right, where a screaming volley hits me straight in the face. "Fuck off!" Well I wasn't counting on the fat bloke jumping up and down waving his fist to wish me a happy birthday. He didn't look that type. An elderly grey-haired woman seated next to him smiles, not sneeringly but apologetically. They call this 'the beautiful game' but it's obvious they've never been here before.

We get closer to the tunnel that leads to the dressing rooms, and the familiar sound of boot-studs clattering against the tarmac echoes around the old brick tunnel like knackered horses on their way to the slaughterhouse. I'm superstitious, so I'm always the last one out of the dressing room and the last one back in. "Shut the fuckin' door behind you," shouts the Gaffer, Paul 'Scully' McKewen. He has an aggressive Glaswegian accent, and it sounds even more aggressive now.

Just forty-five minutes earlier the dressing room was filled with laughter and confidence, rocking to the sounds of 80's club classics. Now it feels more like an overcrowded South American prison cell. It's long and narrow, with thin strips of dark worn wood forming the benches. Faded white tiles cover the walls and at the end of the room there's a large round clock, like the ones we had in school. It leans annoyingly off-axis to the left at 3:52. I turn my head to straighten it up, the long fluorescent lamps above us flickering.

The gaffer's tall, and he stands at the clock end of the dressing room with both hands in his tracksuit-top. He sizes everyone up as we come in one by one, ready to dissect us. I'm the last one to sit down, there's fifteen of us in here now. Like a rectangular clockface starting at one o clock he works his way around the benches. I'm roughly at eight 'o clock between a door to my right, and 'Spider' Paul Delaney to my left. Spider's our masterful midfielder, a unique talent with a very particular skill for scaling high walls. He's just done 18 months for burglary, and is due back in court on Monday morning. He even turned up for one game wearing an electronic tag on his ankle and had to sneak off early to get back before his curfew. He's also got an eye for the ladies; not the kind of bloke you'd want your daughter to bring home. A lovable rogue, but a rogue, nonetheless. Then there's 'Cookie' directly opposite. Fat Pat Cook, our Goalkeeper, he's half Irish and half Jamaican. His big problem is spacial awareness and an obsession for pizza and crisps - both at the same time. Two of the three goals they scored were his fault; one went straight through his hands and the other straight through his legs. If I was being unkind, I'd say the third one was his fault as well, but seeing that just a week earlier his wife Brenda left him a *Dear John* and up and left him with three kids for her toy boy lover, it would be a bit harsh.

"And you, you worthless piece of trash, what the fuck you playing at? Call yourself a Goalkeeper? I've seen more fuckin' movement in a brick wall. No wonder your wife left you if that performance is anything to go by!"

Cookie's sitting arched over with his arms on his knees, staring straight at the floor.

"Are you listening to me, you fat git?" The Gaffer kicks his ankle.

"Yes Gaffer." Cookie's head jolts up and he recoils backwards, clenching his teeth against the pain. "Sorry Gaffer, it won't happen again."

"Aye, I know it won't happen again, 'cos you ain't fuckin' going out for the second half sunshine. You can start getting changed now. Go on, get the fuck out of my sight!"

Cookie slopes off with his head down through the chipped blue door next to me that's marked *showers* in back felt tip.

"Yogi, put your gloves on. You're in for the second half, and be quick about it." He dips into his tracksuit pocket, pulls out a bottle of pills, and empties some into his palm before swallowing the lot.

The only sound is the ticking that mirrors the movement of the clock's second-hand. One-two-three-four. I count five ticks before Billy Eels pipes-up. "Come on boys, pull your fucking fingers out. What's the matter with ya? You're playing like a bunch of wankers - it ain't Christmas yet you know." Eels's the Captain. The Gaffer's favourite. The star striker pin-up. A bit of a wide-boy with the gift of the gab, square chinned, broad shouldered and everything in perfect proportion. Captain Perfect, although his performance was far from that this time round. But as usual, he gets away with it. Maybe he's the son the Gaffer wishes he had. He turns on Spider. "And I don't know what you were playing at."

Spider holds his palms out. "What the fuck you looking at me for?"

"That ball was on. I would have been clean through."

"Bollocks! They were all over you."

"You should open your eyes. Maybe if you turned up for training and got a good night's sleep instead of plotting your next job, smoking weed and jumping in bed with different birds you might get your game back on track, mate."

"Nothing wrong with my game, you big poof."

Spider's got a quick temper, and he launches for Eels's throat with both hands, but Eelsy stands firm and swats him into the wall like a fly. The room erupts and everyone piles in, shouting and screaming to break them apart like the end of a championship boxing fight in Last Vegas after the final bell. Lucky for spider, as he's about six inches shorter and half his opponent's weight.

"Pack it in the lot of ya and sit down!" screams the Gaffer.

"I'll fucking have you," spider shouts.

"Yeah, whenever you're ready."

"I said sit down and shut up, or I'll kick the shit out of all of ya."

Everyone sits back on the benches, but with the sight of little spider bouncing off Eelsy like a rubber ball I can feel a smirk coming on. I lower my head and press my lips together to stop it, trembling as I try to hold it in, but the Gaffer catches my eye.

"And what are you smirking at smart arse? Who the fuck do you think you are, Pele? Too fuckin' cocky. If I've told you once, I've told you a million times; you take another penalty like that again I'll fuckin' throttle you myself, comprende?"

It's my turn but I don't bother looking up. The stench of cigarettes and alcohol on his breath goes so deep into the back of my nose as he leans over me I can taste it in my mouth. He wipes his hair from his forehead.

"You're just a poser son. I know you think your too good for this team, don't you? Well I'm fuckin' telling you sunshine, your ass is grass if you don't -"

There's a double knock at the door. "Time," someone shouts from outside.

Thank God for that. The half-time interrogation's over.

"You bunch of tarts got us into this fuckin' mess, and you's lot had better get us out of it, or don't even think about coming back 'cos your fuckin' lives won't be worth living. Comprende?" He opens the dressing room door, stands by it and screws us out one by one as we file past him like condemned prisoners being ordered back to work. Can we really turn this mess around?

I'm the last one out of the dressing room.

"Shut the fuckin' door behind you."

...o jogo bonito – Pele
...the beautiful game - Pele

GHOST STORIES

R.E. Charles

Don't pick up hitch-hikers.

Never, ever.

It's the number one rule.

Ghosts are out there, everywhere, in all guises, along with knife wielding mother-fixated psychos, mask wearing sex-killers, insane Austrian surgeons and game-devising torturers. But with a little common sense they can all be avoided – unless you are particularly unlucky. So never stray from rule number one, for to do that is the most proven way of becoming victim to any of the above.

But what else can you do? As it happens, quite a lot.

Don't decide to spend the weekend with a few friends in any kind of remote cabin deep inside the woods. Or by a lake. Or on a boat on the lake. And don't take the piss out of the local hillbilly you ask directions from on your way there; he may just seem to be a strange but harmless bumpkin with a lazy eye who spits gloop out the side of his mouth, but in reality he probably has a basement full of skulls and a deep sense of confusion over his relationship with his mother/sister/brother, any of whom he might have slept with, married or killed. Probably all three.

Don't be a teenager. Especially a Colgate grinning cheer-leading Prom Queen, or her football captain boyfriend, Todd. If you do happen to be a Prom Queen or a Todd, and you find yourself in a big house with hopes of losing your virginity, for Christ's sake don't go off on your own to see what that strange noise is (with a candle or a torch because there's been a power cut). Especially if that noise is coming from the basement. It is so fucking annoying when you do that!

Don't play with Ouija boards for a bit of a laugh. Especially in that old house on the hill where that bloke slaughtered his family. It's not worth it, even if you don't believe in ghosts. When your friends are daring you, and making chicken noises, just go home, have a cup of tea and watch Strictly, or Game of Thrones, anything at all . . . perhaps with the exception of something hosted by Ant and Dec. You'd have to weigh that one up.

I could go on. There are so many ways to keep yourself from harm. It's so easy, in fact, it makes me wonder if some people go out of their way to be haunted, hunted, deserted and terrorised. You just have to see the light – and I think I've just seen mine. A pair of lights actually, slowing, slowing. Is he really going to stop and offer me a lift? I suppose I should be grateful; drivers like him are rare.

Not everybody can see ghosts.

IN SEARCH OF R. E. CHARLES

Raymond Little

Prolific author of contemporary fiction. Philosopher. Libertine. Playwright. Political agitator. Chess Grandmaster. Fashion guru. Self-taught donkey whisperer and the western world's foremost connoisseur on lamb Dhansak.

These are just some of the terms found on the author's self-penned Amazon page that describe this elusive, modern day Renaissance man. But just who is R. E. Charles? Armed with a notepad, more questions than I would find answers to, and a growing sense of inferiority at meeting the man who claims to be a legend, I arrived at his South London home for the rarest of opportunities; the first interview in twenty years granted by this figure who has remained an enigma for much of his artistic career. And physical entry, despite my appointment, was not to be taken for granted. Charles protects his privacy with utmost care.

"Yes?" Two blue eyes peered at me through the six-inch gap of door and frame, the brass security chain between us.

"I have an appointment," I informed him. "An interview." I held up my driver's licence for his perusal. He narrowed his eyes.

"Flip it over," he commanded, his voice deep and authoritative. "Ooh, full licence. Impressive." He raised an eyebrow in a manner for which I could decipher no meaning and stared at me for a full five seconds. "Well?"

"What?"

"Questions of course. Have you come to interview me or am I standing here like an arse for no reason?"

"Well, I was hoping I might come inside."

"Inside?" He seemed outraged at first, but his frown turned by degrees to a smile. "I see they've sent along their best man. I like the way you think, Roger."

"My name's Ray . . ."

"Whatever," he interrupted. "I like you. You are untraditional. Flying under the radar." He lowered his voice. "I dig that."

The door closed for a few seconds to enable him to undo the chain, before he swept it open. He stood before me, a fist resting on each of his hips, his slippered feet planted wide on the carpet. He stood, six feet tall, in a paisley-patterned silken dressing gown. His hair was short and silver, and lines fanned from the corners of his eyes. I recalled the photo on his Amazon page, a shot of him in some paradise, the sun sinking behind a palm tree. He was blond in the picture, and a little slimmer, with no lines on his face, and I wondered just how long ago that photograph had been taken.

"I know what you're thinking." He lifted his chin and looked down the length of his nose at me. "I look much younger in real life."

"Well, erm. Indeed."

"Do you drink tea?" He asked.

"Yes."

"Have you any tea bags?"

I patted my pockets. "Er, no."

"Shame." He turned on his heels. "Come!" He ordered, and I obeyed, following him along the passageway to his living room. "Make yourself comfortable," he said, and I chose an armchair by the bay window. The room was tidy and decorated in lush nineteen-seventies colours and ornaments, which is the mode this year for those in the know.

"Very modern," I said, gazing at his orange and brown circular patterned curtains, meaning to compliment him on his taste. "Have you just refurbished?"

He looked confused for a moment, before widening his eyes. "Oh, yes," he nodded, "that's right, it's all new."

My attention was drawn to a poster of a blonde woman, dressed in tennis whites, her back to the photographer as she lifts one side of the back of her short tennis skirt to scratch her behind. "Is that a statement? Some sort of ironic comment on modern feminism in the *me-too* era?" I asked.

"Me what?" He frowned, then suddenly clapped his hands and pointed at me. "That's right. It's a, erm, statement. It isn't there for titillation of any kind at all."

"Right, good." I retrieved my notepad from my satchel. "Shall we begin?"

He wagged a finger. "What's that?"

I looked at my brown leather bag. "It's for my stuff. You know, notepad, phone, wallet, keys . . ."

"It's a bloody handbag, Roger."

I laughed nervously at his humour. "Well, it isn't what I call it, but . . ."

"I believe in calling a mangle a mangle. And that's a handbag. You need to get a grip, my man."

"I don't think . . ."

He laughed and dropped onto the sofa opposite. "I'm just giving you shit. Take no notice."

I relaxed a little. He was an odd man, certainly, but what else had I been expecting? Genius and unconformity often shine bright on either side of the same blade. "I'd like to start with your earliest known work. You began as a playwright, but changed to novel writing after only one production. Why was that?"

He gazed at the window, a faraway look in his eyes. "There are people in this world, particularly critics, who do not appreciate modernist work. The play also caused a rift between myself and my wife at the time. Though God knows why."

I had already noticed the theatre poster from that long-ago production preserved in a frame, propped under his window. I read the title out loud. "*I Had It Off with Your Sister*."

He sighed. "A lot of no-good came from that play. And not only my divorce. Bad review after bad review, though the public swarmed to it."

"How long did it run?"

"One month. Critics held quite a sway then, as did public decency laws. So I turned to the novel."

I jotted some notes. "Your early novels acquired quite a cult status, despite some reviewers calling them impenetrable. *Canary Hunting Under Hammersmith Bypass* was your debut as a novelist, and typical of the difficult themes you would come to tackle. Where exactly do you find your ideas?"

Charles chortled. "Does a dog know where to find a bone? It's like Schrodinger's Hat, Roger; a complete mystery. Nobody knows which room he left that damned hat in. Even Stephen Hawking couldn't figure that one out."

I admit I was as confused at this juncture as he claimed the great physicist would have been, but let it pass. "Other titles fared as badly with critics," I said. "*Traffic Warden Civil War*, *Christmas With Dave Including Pudding*, *Extremist Nuns' Olympics* and *The Sunday Afternoon Cat-Taunting Society of Irkutsk*."

"Critics can go poke their heads up their arses and jump in a drain," he growled.

"There were also the two plagiarism suits against you."

"As I said at the time, any similarities between those novels and the plaintiffs were coincidental."

"So, *The Michelangelo Code* and *The Curious Incident of the Frog in the Night-Time* were completely original?"

"Of course." His stare, though not quite icy, was definitely gathering frost. I decided to finish with some quick-fire questions. "According to your biography on

Goodreads, you have been quite active in the political arena. What do you think of Brexit?"

"It's a must. Usually porridge, or a fry up. And kippers for lunch."

I pushed on regardless. "Donald Trump?"

Confusion flashed in his eyes. "He's cute, I suppose, in his little sailor's outfit. He should wear trousers, though. That's pretty disgusting for a kid's cartoon, even if he is a duck. What is all this? I thought you were going to ask me some serious questions!"

I looked at the notes I'd taken, which seemed to make as much sense as this man's work and career, and found myself at a loss as for how to move forward.

"You seem perplexed," he purred. "Let me give you some advice. If you want to understand me, you must first deconstruct me, in order to reconstruct me." He looked suddenly pleased with himself and shook his finger at my pad. "That's good, write it down, write it down, damn it!"

I did, and took my leave. Maybe he was right, I reflected on my way to the bus stop. Maybe all I did need to understand this man was in my notes. Right now though, I was as confused as Stephen Hawking must have been in his search for Schrodinger's Hat.

DOGMEAT

H.C. Johnston

Have you ever met a Shih Tzu?

Look, you don't meet one, you fend it off. Don't believe the PR nonsense about friendly outgoing toy dogs. They're friendly like a shark and outgoing like a hyena. And a toy like a man-trap.

So naturally my boss's daughter Mitzi, teenage trend-setter, had to have one. "They're so cute, Athlone!" she mooned. "But you're a Man, and Men don't notice."

And that, I think, is how the mess really started.

Mitzi expected me to sort her dog issue as I'm the go-to guy for the Schmidt family, whether private or business, no job too small, wet, or dirty. What the Schmidts want, I see to it that they shall have, discreetly and silently.

A friend owned the animal Mitzi had set her heart on, Baby or Zhuzhi or some such - the girl, not the dog. I offered a king's ransom, but the pooch was not for sale. Then Mitzi located a litter-brother, "so I rule and Athlone sucks!" and she called the critter Trisong after a Tibetan emperor. How are the mighty fallen; from monarch to mall-rat's pet.

Like a true emperor, Trisong does not care where it shits and expects to be pampered at all hours of the day and night. If service is not up to its exacting standards it whines. Loudly.

But Trisong made Mitzi happy, and this was a Good Thing in the eyes of her father, Frank. Because Mitzi was at the awkward age.

Now, as far as I know, Mitzi has been at the awkward age since conception, and that's not quite as snotty as it sounds. How do you solve a problem like Mitzi?

Frank is not now and never has been a conventional family man, much though he likes the image. Frank is a man of business: his household is not his primary concern and he is refreshingly honest about that. His current wife, La

Baronne, is well aware she is not the centre of his universe. She treats her position professionally and does that to the best of her considerable ability.

But for Frank, Mitzi could do no wrong. I saw that she was not just the pet of the moment, but most unusually, Frank recognised her as another human being. And, as any kid of nine or so will do, she played this up for all she was worth.

So where did Mitzi come from? When I started working for Frank, I tried to track this down: she was certainly not from La Baronne's ice-cold womb. Was Mitzi a vanity adoption?

Bernard, then Frank's secretary and gopher, went pale. "For God's sake, man, never even hint that," he said. "She's blood of his blood, never forget."

"Maybe a test-tube? She can't be a clone, can she?"

Bernard shivered again. "No, a natural process," squeezing the word 'natural' out in a sort of croak. But, in the end, it was no real business of mine, and there was no point asking Frank himself: Frank does not do unnecessary questions. A couple of weeks later, Bernard wasn't there, and the rumour was he'd asked Frank once too often why he visited Bucharest so much. (I have no idea. Frank does not go there now. He has scribbled it out of the map of Europe above his desk.)

I know which questions not to ask. I rub along so well in Frank's organisation, I am practically shiny. Mitzi might as well have been reconstituted from a freeze-dried Instant Daughter mix: not my problem.

Spot the mistake. Yes, I took my eye off the ball. Because recently the low-register persistent whine which tells you that Mitzi is a) approaching and b) dissatisfied with life, started to get louder.

She wanted a slice of the action. Well, probably not in reality, because that would mean work. Frank puts in eighteen-hour days, while Mitzi has the concentration span of a gnat. She wanted a slice of the status. She wanted to be part of Daddy's world.

"She is Frank's heir, I suppose," I said to Gerry, an accountant.

Gerry snorted. "It's not The Godfather. She's not Michael Corleone or Sofia Coppola. If she's good enough, Frank will bring her on the team in due course, and if she isn't –"

Gerry, being an accountant, has no imagination. If she wasn't, we could look forward to an infinite future of whining and moaning, and all the vendettas and unpleasantness that she could devise, which, given the family traits -

So when Frank did say no, and she went into a galactic-scale sulk, even he could see Mitzi had to be distracted. Cue shopping trips to Paris and the must-have objects like the sports car and the mutt.

But then her moaning took an unexpected turn. She was developing an Unhappy Past.

"You know, Athlone, it's hard not to know who you are," she said one day, as I drove her back to her school. "I mean, who am I, really?"

"You are really my boss's daughter, you are a student at the Lake Academy, this is the start of term and you will be an ex-student if I don't get you there in time." I pressed harder on the Bentley's accelerator. She was grounded from using her Lexus after an incident with the gardener's goat and a fire-engine.

"It's so confusing," she said. "I mean, when I go really Deep, like my Core Being, who am I? I mean, like, we've all got these really ancient – er – things that make us who we are – er - what are they?"

"Genes, my little coelacanth."

"Yeah, and like they - influence us. Like your star sign but, like, deeper. And if there's, like, you know, Tragedy, or whatever in your Past then you have to Work Through your Hideous Fate and then you get reborn as a better thing, like a – a –"

"Shih Tzu?"

She actually brightened. "Yes! So I could come back as Trisong - sweetie-sweetie-sweetie-" I should be plain she was talking to the dog at this point. "And then I could come back as something really cool."

Well, it was an unusual view of the hierarchy of reincarnation. I could not resist asking. "So what would you come back as?"

"Like, a really big robot? Like, you know, Transformers?"

Oof. "I don't think machines count. I think it has to be flesh and blood."

"Really?" She was genuinely disappointed. "OMG!"

"Anyway, how about concentrating on this life before you get to the next ones? Such as getting good exam results?" God, I was beginning to sound like a real parent.

"But Athlone, I can't! Not if I don't Really Know Who I Am! Who knows what terrible crimes I must avenge and what dark hidden depths I must explore before I can be ready for my Great Task!"

Things became a touch clearer. Mitzi is no reader but even she can get her head around the latest tale from Marvel. Since comics went 'adult' the world has been full of adolescents seeking a quest for which their undiscovered superpowers make them uniquely suited. Mitzi was exploring her inner Batman.

In any other kid, this is a phase. But it did strike me that whatever is lurking in Mitzi's deep, murky gene pool, it has a big dose of Frank, and that is a place probably best left undisturbed. Mitzi Not Knowing Who She Is pales into insignificance beside Mitzi Knowing Exactly Who She Is.

However, all went quiet after she was delivered to the school, apart from the usual midnight phone-calls because a girl was mean, or a teacher was 'dorky', or the groundsman gave her the creeps. I had to explain, yet again and with feeling, that my role did not encompass murder on demand for just any member of Frank's family, however irritating the mark might be. The school also sent the dog back over a 'behavioural problem' (translation, shits all over the dean's study), leading to a short debate about what to do with it while Mitzi was away. I was for a quick execution and replacement with identical pooch if she noticed the absence. But La Baronne nixed this.

"It's Mitzi's pet, she has to decide," she said. "You look after Trisong, Athlone, you need a faithful companion in your life."

I think that was a joke, but it can be very hard to tell with La Baronne.

Trisong and I ignored each other as best we could. It ate, it shat, it slept on its velvet cushion, an estate hand took it walkies, and it snarled if I came within five paces. And it yapped. Continuously. Until it could see my nerves were fraying, when it would howl.

But there were fewer enquiries from Mitzi about darling Trisong. With luck, by the end of term Trisong would be just so last year and I could get rid of the mutt.

Again, spot the mistake. Because now there was a Trisong-shaped gap in Mitzi's life, which meant that the Task and the Question of Who She Was loomed larger. Suddenly she wanted to see family birth certificates, presumably just in case she had been kidnapped at birth and was really a princess.

This was relayed to me by a worried Frank. "What does she want to know for? What do I care who my grandad was?" He was rattled and upset. "Paperwork! Bloody paperwork! I'm here, what more does she want?"

There was, of course, a much bigger problem. Even if Frank has a birth certificate, the chances of it saying 'Frank Schmidt' are nil. That's not the way Frank or his family operate. It is not altogether true that Frank does not care about 'paperwork' but it is certainly true that he does not want it in anyone else's hands, including his ever-loving daughter. Once you can pin a man like Frank down to names and places, no good can come of it - for him, anyway. Frank told Mitzi his papers were lost in some big fire in Hendon, and as his people were illiterate scum, there would not be much to find anyway. So there was no point looking. La Baronne said that true aristocracy never bothered with petty bureaucracy.

But then Mitzi started sending us bills for 'searches' through an outfit called Hereward Connections. They were for a couple of hundred quid a go, and seemed to be about churches.

"I hope she hasn't got religion," said Frank. "One of my aunts went funny that way. Gave all her money to nuns, silly cow."

"I think that's highly unlikely," I said. "Mitzi doesn't strike me as the contemplative type."

"Can't you get this bloody thing to stop slavering on me?" said Frank. Trisong had taken a fancy to him, but Frank did not repay the affection.

"Trisong!" I waggled my finger. And, like a jet-propelled ferret, Trisong launched itself at my hand. The wound was relatively small, no stitches needed, and it's what I'm paid for.

"Athlone, find out what these guys are up to. I don't want my Mitzi taken for a ride by -" and here Frank went into a colourful but basically obscene description of those afflicted with religious faith.

*

Hereward Connections were in Prickwillow. No, I hadn't heard of it, either. Its fame has not spread beyond the flat, featureless farmland of Ely, in the most flat, featureless part of East Anglia, a place that makes quite a speciality of featureless. Even when you get to Prickwillow, it's the sort of village where it is quite hard to tell you have arrived.

The company did have a website. They offered genealogy services, so that was one worry abated: nothing overtly religious. But Frank was still not happy. "Just sort them out, Athlone."

Hereward Connections turned out to be based in a terraced Victorian cottage. The door was opened by a harassed man in his mid-thirties, with spectacles and the sort of haircut your wife gives you to save money. Beyond him in the back of the house, someone was cooking cabbage. I hoped.

"How can I -" he said. Then he caught sight of the Bentley. "Are you lost?"

"Not if you're Mr Fuller? My name is Athlone. I understand you've been doing genealogy searches for a member of my employer's family? Miss Mitzi Zamlinsky."

(It's a long story.)

He smiled. "Oh, Mitzi! Such a nice kid. Yes, we're beginning to make some headway."

"I was intrigued by all the church names on your documentation."

"Oh, that's the parish registers, you can only get so far with official records and the Census and so forth. Come in, come in."

The house was small, and dark, and stank of cabbage, and every wall in the tiny living room was covered in books and files. A battered computer desk in the corner was submerged in cabling, a laptop and three elderly computer monitors. "All satellite, costs a fortune," he grumbled. "Simply cannot get a good internet connection, been complaining for years. Here, sit down." He knocked some papers off a shabby armchair onto the ancient shag-pile carpet. "Would you like tea?"

All right, it was beginning to feel like clubbing a baby seal.

"We - Mitzi's family - appreciate that she wants to trace her background but her father worries, she has her school work and as you know, every family has its secrets and what you find out in these projects -"

"Is not always what you want to know." He grinned. "Oh, we recognise that, Mr -"

"Just Athlone. Quite. No point in raking up the past, is there."

"Absolutely. I did explain that to Mitzi, but so far there's no murderers." He called to the back room." Janey, our guest won't, but I'd like a tea."

"No murderers at all?" That did surprise me.

He laughed, wheezily. "You sound disappointed! Most families are very ordinary. Initially we're tracing her mother's people. It's a shame we can't ask the lady, but I gather she's not with us."

"Her mother?"

"Well, yes." He smiled at me as if I were just a little hard of thinking.

"I didn't realise Mitzi -"

Janey chose this moment to come in with the tea for her husband: a mousy woman with a fierce set to her mouth. "Oh, everyone's got a mother, Mr Athlone. I'd take a bet even you've got one!" Then she turned on her heel and marched back to the kitchen.

Fuller leaned forward. "Sorry about that, Janey doesn't quite appreciate the fascination of family history. Not like us!" He toasted me with his tea.

"Her mother? So that would be -" imagination runs riot - the chair - the rug - the tea - "the Browns?"

He looked puzzled. "No, the Kelseys, very old local name. A shame we don't have much detail about her, thins down the lines to pursue, you see." He grinned.

So I got out my club and I clubbed him to death.

No, I didn't. I explained that Mitzi's father did not want her to be distracted, and we should draw a line under everything found so far.

"I'm sure you understand, Mr Fuller. If Mitzi wants to take it up again after exams -"

"Oh, I understand, Mr Athlone." He grinned. "On ice, it is."

"I'm sorry if this means we've wasted your time."

"No difficulty. As it happens, I have another client who needs the same records." He grinned again.

"The same? Who -"

"Oh, I'm afraid I have to keep my clients confidential." And he meant it, the bastard.

We shook hands and parted. I made a note to find a local tradesman who could get in and search - no, not the slightest point in searching that rat's nest - get in and persuade Mr Fuller and the lovely Janey - maybe money would sweeten the wife - bribe her and kick him into touch, in a two-pronged - but the way she looked at him, she'd see his throat cut quite happily. It's not as simple as people think, this gig. Anyway, get in, and not leave until he had the name of the other client.

*

I told Frank that Mitzi's search had been stopped, and nothing had come up about him.

"Athlone, why is this animal screwing my foot? It's not nice."

"Trisong! Finger!"

Still no stitches.

Kelsey. Mitzi's mother was called Kelsey. The name rang no bells. Had Mitzi seen her birth certificate? Was that what had triggered all the 'who am I, where am I, why am I here' stuff? Hardly the sort of thing that's just knocking around, at least, mine certainly isn't, and of course neither is Frank's. I broke it to him that Mitzi might have found her mother's name.

"Yeah, well, that's the new passport, innit. When she hit sixteen, got her one, you need a birth certificate for that. I'm keeping her legal. No big secret. Catherine's her mum. Nobody's heard from her in a dog's age. Talking of which, why is this one sucking my sock?"

He passed this all off very lightly, which puzzled me. This was Frank, normally so paranoid about people 'knowing things' that all outside communications were encoded and paperwork was not only shredded but obliterated. Very curious.

In fact, not only did Frank not want to talk about it, La Baronne shut me down before I even opened my mouth. It was a non-topic. The tradesman had done his best but Fuller proved to be asthmatic and went into shock easily, while Janey was a dab hand with an old tyre lever and could shriek like a hurricane. No information there, either.

So when I next saw Mitzi, I hoped she had just forgotten the entire business. There was a parent's fair at the school where you were supposed to meet the teachers and discuss your lovely offspring. As ever, I was pretend-daddy for the day.

Which is when I first saw Neil. Damn. Trisong had been replaced all right. Mitzi had graduated from dogs to boys.

The dean was very affable; Mitzi was doing well, she was a very methodical girl if a task interested her although kick-starting her concentration could be a little tough.

"Who are the boys in blazers?"

"Oh, from our associate school. We like to create a good social mix for our girls! They're helping us out for their Society in Transition module."

In other words, they were being waiters. Mitzi flirted girlishly with a thin ginger lad, whose nose approached the size of a traffic cone and whose chin was chiefly remarkable for the amount of acne fitted on it, until she spotted me.

I took her aside. "Are you nuts? Who's he?"

"His name's Neil and he's very, very rich," she said. "So daddy can't complain. He's a Viscount."

Neil decided to wade in. "I say, Mitzi, is this chap bothering you?"

"Silly!" said Mitzi. "This is Athlone. He's one of Daddy's people, he doesn't matter." She turned her back on me and marched Neil towards the cake-stall.

"Ouch," said a voice beside me. "They can be so annoying when they show off."

The voice belonged to a woman in her early forties, who had a refreshing lack of the air of hyper-wealth. "Hello, I'm Kay Lincoln. I'm one of Mitzi's tutors."

"How do you do, I'm – not Mitzi's dad."

She laughed. "We rarely see Mr Schmidt, I gather. Are you -"

"No, I'm not family either. I work for Mr Schmidt. A personal assistant."

"Would you like some tea?"

A very pleasant lady.

Of course, I had to alert Frank to Viscount Neil, but after consulting the Almanac de Gotha and the Web, I established that he was indeed very rich and not only had a proper title but would inherit an even bigger one when his daddy popped off.

"Well, she's picking them well, wouldn't you say, Athlone?" Frank almost seemed proud.

"But what if it gets serious?"

"Nah, this is just playing around. It won't last. Blimey, you don't know much about girls!"

Actually, it was not the state of Mitzi's heart that I was concerned about. It was whether Neil's family would be terribly delighted to be connected to Frank, and how far they would go to track Frank down. I needed to know more about them.

Well, I did know a genealogist.

*

Fuller opened the door only after I knocked on it for five minutes and passed a note through the letterbox. Eventually, with much scrabbling at locks, I was allowed in.

"Sorry to hear about your problem," I said. "This is very remote, I suppose."

"Hideous," he muttered. "You can see how much damage they did."

Actually, I couldn't. It's very hard to damage thirty-year old shag-pile carpet and moquette furniture from the Ark.

"Did you find out what it was about?"

"No, he just yelled. The police say they go for cash."

I made a note to take the tradesman off my termination list. He had kept his cool and left no obvious clues, even though the job had gone south.

"Slightly unconventional request," I said. "This family is quite famous in their way, but I need to know more - nothing off-colour, just the broader picture." I passed Fuller a printout with a photo of Neil and his parents. "Have you heard of them?"

"No," said Fuller, without a trace of a start or a micro-expression. Neil's lot were not his mystery client, at least.

I smiled helpfully. "I hope Mitzi didn't give you a hard time after my last visit."

"I had to tell her about her mother, of course."

I strained every nerve to be as casual as possible. "Oh? What?"

"Well, that's she's still alive. Seemed to come as a surprise, but you can't keep that sort of information from a child, can you?" His big-eyed gaze was innocence itself, like a baby seal.

So I clubbed him.

No, I didn't.

"Her mother? You know, the family did rather lose track of her."

"I can't talk about my clients, Mr Athlone, you know that."

*

Her mother was the client. As I drove back to base, certainty grew like a vast mushroom-cloud. Mitzi's mother was looking for her. Frank had to know.

"Oh," he said. "Right. That creature's been pissing in my slippers."

Trisong looked up cheerfully, then it saw me and –

So, needed a stitch.

But in contrast to Frank's careful unconcern, La Baronne went straight into icy wariness. "Really? I wonder why."

There was no good answer. I presumed the woman had been paid off or scared off in Frank's inimitable manner. There had been no sign of her for at least thirteen years. She wanted something; Mitzi, the daughter she left behind? Or what Mitzi represented; wealth, power, a way back into Frank's life? In which case, what price La Baronne?

All this was very destabilising.

Mitzi was troubled in reality, as well as in the Great Quest sense, which started to come out at half term. She was playing with the dog. "I wonder what it's like to have a mother," she said.

"Tell you what, you can have mine. Foul-mouthed old bitch who couldn't get rid of me fast enough."

"No, I mean a real mother."

The truth: a hell of a lot tougher than you've had it. If the mother had a fantasy, so did Mitzi. The quickest way out of the whole mess might be to leave them together in a locked room. "Well, you had one, but she's not here now, and-"

"Kay says mothers always have a connection with their children no matter what. You can be the worst mother in the world and still it's there, you can't do anything about it."

"Kay?"

"Mrs. Lincoln. My social studies tutor. She's really nice."

Kay. Very pleasant lady.

"That's a sweet idea but it isn't always true, you know."

Which was worse, the next question, or Mitzi's dead-shark eyes when she asked me?

"You don't believe in love, do you, Athlone?"

This was not a sixteen-year-old girl being emotional and accusing, but Frank's heir sizing me up for weaknesses. Careful, now.

"I think people get it mixed up with an awful lot of other stuff. It sounds like a good idea but life's more complicated than that."

"So you don't think I really love Neil?"

"I'm sure you're very -" The dead eyes watched me so carefully. Fond? Friendly? In lust? "Very wrapped up in each other. But I'm not sure you know each other well enough yet -"

Well, blow me down and call me Aunt Agony.

"Right," said Mitzi. "And what about my mother?"

"Look, the last time she saw you, you were a very little girl. You've – developed - a lot since then."

"So she won't love me any more?" Flat, toneless. A test, with no right answer.

Mitzi busied herself with the dog, which chased its tail so prettily and yapped so humorously now the mistress was home. "Kay says mothers don't care about that. Unconditional love. It's like loyalty. It's there, or it isn't, and mothers have it." And that was the end of the conversation.

*

Frank was pleased with the run-down on Neil's family. There was money, land and titles, and a couple of really fruity scandals for further research should insurance be needed. Although this would not be by Hereward Connections. Fuller was even greener and shorter of breath when I collected his findings than the last time.

"A job well done," I said. "I hope Mitzi's mother is having equal success?"

"Well, all wrapped up, really - Oh." He stopped himself, looking like a hamster caught in flagrante. I laughed lightly, and we parted on a handshake.

Frank told Mitzi that Viscount Neil was all right in his book. Almost immediately, the lad began to decline in her favours. Blimey, how had I missed that one? At the school garden party, her dead eyes were casting around for the next object of affection. She's a real chip off the old block.

I looked for Kay, who might have hippy-dippy ideas about mother-love but had been pleasant company. But the dean frowned. "I really can't help you," he said. "She resigned very suddenly and seems to have left the country. Very inconvenient, I can tell you."

"What a shame."

"Mrs Lincoln was a real find, but apparently there was a hidden factor there. A shame, as you say."

*

"Mitzi, when you were tracing your family -"

She didn't answer. She was playing tug of war with Trisong and an old sock.

"Did you find what you were looking for?"

She shrugged. "That's so - It doesn't matter. It's what's here now that matters."

"Not even for your Great Quest?"

She shrugged again. "I'm superior to all that. My quest will find me. Paul says so."

Ah, the latest squeeze. "He sounds sensible."

She sniffed. "It's all in Neechy."

Eh? It took me a good two minutes to work out she meant Nietsche. But that was a problem for another day. As long as it's not Mein Kampf.

"I was sorry to hear about Mrs Lincoln."

She almost started. "Who? Oh, her. Yeah. Yeah. She was really stupid, you know? All that thing about mothers. Really stupid."

Whoa. That was a strong emotional reaction from my little hammerhead.

"Stand still, Athlone. Trisong! Attack!" Which the mutt did, to Mitzi's glee. "You know, dogs are so great, like unconditional love? Like, they do whatever you want them to and they really just know who's on your side."

I could not suppress a yelp: after months of trial and error, Trisong had located a nerve just above my Achilles' tendon. "Youch! I'm on your side, Mitzi!"

"Not everybody is," she said, matter of fact. "You know, Neil was sweet but like, Paul's got more -"

"Money?"

"Smarts," she said. "He can carry things through. Like you do for Daddy."

A compliment, however back-handed.

"And Neil couldn't?"

"Sort of, but he kind of bottled out a lot."

I later found that Viscount Neil had suffered a 'nervous breakdown' a few weeks before and was last known at a very private secure retreat in Oregon. He had been discovered in the school gym with one of his father's shotguns, but so incoherent it was not clear if he was suicidal, murderous, or both. Ammunition was missing, too, and never found.

And neither was Mrs. Lincoln. Eventually the police reported that they had 'concerns for her safety'. Mrs. Lincoln - nee Kelsey. And Kay was short for Katharine.

How had the conversation gone? Had Kay bounced in with, 'I'm your mummy, and things are going to change around here?' Or maybe, 'I'm your mummy, now you must love me?' Unconditional love can cut both ways.

Or perhaps, 'I have things to tell you, uncomfortable things about your father, and I had to go away, but I don't care any more and I'll fight that man for you, if we have to live in a hovel –'

Or any other romantic notion. I don't think Kay was in it for the money, this was not a shake-down. There might have been guilt and that terrible instinct that ties a mother to its offspring. There might have been curiosity. I can't know.

The only clue came a couple of months later. Mitzi was playing with Trisong - give the mutt credit, it can always please its exacting mistress - when she said, "Dogs know."

"Know what?"

"I know when someone's on my side, because Trisong likes them. He likes Daddy."

"But he hates me, my little Borgia."

"No, he likes playing with you. He never really bites you."

"Four stitches might be evidence to the contrary, my modern Zenobia."

"Who?"

"Google it." If that was evidence of affection, I could live without. "So who doesn't he like?"

She sniffed. "He hated Mrs. Lincoln. He always barked like, really fiercely?"

Maybe Kay had not said anything. Maybe trial by Shih Tzu had sealed her fate, delivered by a half-mad lad with a shotgun.

Just dogmeat.

A FOREIGN AFFAIR

Gwynneth Pedler

She looked down at her feet which were thick with mud, and cast a glance at her surroundings. The road, little more than an alleyway, was in poor repair. Missing drain covers, open culverts and pot holes sat like traps for the unwary traveller. A recent thunderstorm had added its contribution to this run-down, slippery passageway. Her shoes were now squelching with mud, making it difficult for her to keep upright. In this little backwater the weak lamplight revealed derelict buildings covered with trailing vines and fig trees. An occasional dimly lit window seemed to be the only evidence of civilisation in this chaotic and turbulent city.

A sudden darkness befell her as one of the frequent power cuts took away any sense of security. The hairs on the back of her neck were at full alert. The acrid smell of raw sewage filled her nostrils, and air pollution invaded her mouth. The feel of her torch with its feeble light brought little comfort, and the sound of an approaching car was enough to fill her with terror. She flattened herself against a fence as the car raced by, throwing up even more mud. Here she was in the poorest country in Europe where serious crime was rife, alone, cold, dirty and vulnerable. She wondered if this was all a bad dream.

She slowed her breathing to clear her mind, and had a vision of how it all began, with a phone call . . .

Lying in her peaceful garden, glass of wine beside her and a book lying open on her lap, Gwynneth's serenity was disrupted by the shrill ring of the telephone. With a tut of irritation she answered with a curt "hello.".

The quiet voice of a woman came over the line. "Am I speaking to Gwynneth Pedler?"

"Yes."

"I've been given your name as someone who would be able to help me."

Gwynneth settled a little, her curiosity aroused.

"I work for a Charity that supplies aid to Albania," the woman said, "and a project has arisen that I think you might be able to help me with. Could we meet?"

Thoughts rushed through Gwynneth's head. Albania? From what she knew, it was a country with lots of unrest, and probably not safe. She hesitated, but never able to resist a challenge she agreed to meet the woman.

And so it was that one week later, over a cup of coffee (wine or even G&T would have been better), they sat chatting about Albania and the difficulties it faced with a recent change of Government. She worried whether she was ready for the mammoth challenge presented to her.

"The Charity has received a grant to open a Nursery school in the centre of Tirana and we are looking for an experienced person to head it, train the teachers, and be responsible for equipping the school. Would you be willing to take this on?"

The woman was persuasive but Gwynneth needed more information. The little she knew about Albania suggested it was alien territory to her; would she cope with the hardships she would encounter?

The following week involved a frenzied search for information; maps, leaflets and books littered the floor, desk, table, and every surface possible.

For the next few days, Gwynneth's emotions were like a seesaw, one day up with excitement, her mind full of plans, and the next full of fear and doubts. The week flew by, and a knock on the door announced decision day had arrived; what would her answer be? Was it a positive day, or was it a negative day of doubts and fears? Would heart win over head or head over heart? But her face said it all; she really wanted go. Her concerns brushed aside, she signed the contract. Frantic preparations and arrangements were made to keep her house safe during her absence, and departure day dawned at last.

As the plane took off, Gwynneth looked down and watched England fade from sight. She thought of her friends and family and the comfortable life she was leaving behind in exchange for hardship and challenge.

HOW OLD IS OLD?

Fay Brown

In the UK the term "old" is related to terms such as *aged, elderly, past the sell by date, fragile.* The Oxford Dictionary defines old amongst other terms as *made or built long ago, belonging to the past; former etc.* Hence, it's sometimes difficult when referring to the elderly to avoid the connotation that they are outdated, old fashioned, of another age, and in some cases of no value.

We assume, and stereotype old people to be frail, weak, lonely, unfit, unwell, isolated and not fit for work . . . yet here in Olhao, a beautiful Mediterranean community located in Southern Portugal on the Algarve famous for its fishing port and harbour, things are a little different. Here, "old people" seems to take on another meaning; I'm seeing "old" men and women looking healthy, vibrant, happy, fit, soaking up the sun, enjoying life with their partners, families, grandchildren and friends. Experiencing the good weather in shorts, swimming trunks, sunglasses, trilby sunhats. They are enjoying life to the full.

I'm seeing "old" men and women running businesses, working to make a living either as fishermen, shop owners or other professions. So I ask myself, "what does *old* really mean?" Does it mean different things to different cultures? Does good weather, healthy food and family networks change the definition in different countries? For example, I'm on the beach and I've just seen an elderly man come out of the sea in his skimpy black swimming trunks, taking pictures of his family including his daughter (or is it his grand-daughter?) in her bikini. He must be at least 70 years old judging by the different generations of family on the beach with him, yet he's got the suntanned body of a 30-year-old, despite his wrinkles, grey hair and bent arthritic fingers.

How did it happen that this "old" man has the body of a 30-year-old? Is he an anomaly in Portugal or is he typical of men his age in this beautiful island? I suspect the latter. Wow, what a life to have at his age.

One day my daughter and I got the ferry to one of the small Portuguese islands. While on the ferry I see an "old" English lady intent on her Word search puzzle, sitting opposite her grandson who is listening to music on his expensive Beats wireless headphones. I try to imagine what kind of music he's listening to. Is it via one of the Millennium music apps such as Spotify or iTunes? My Lord, back in the day when I was a teenager they didn't have a digital age where you could simply plug into a music app - how times have changed!

Walking back from the beach along an extended walkway (in the middle of what looks like a mini desert) to meet the ferry, we walk past the villagers' endearing houses. I see another "old" local woman happily crocheting an item for her shop, set up at the front of her house which displays an array of knitted toys. She looks so happy and content. My mind immediately switches to my professional work back in the UK.

Back home I work for a charity supporting old people in an inner-city multi-cultural borough in south London, where I witness a very different experience of what it means to be old. The ages range from 55 to 90 plus. Many I see are lonely, on low incomes, isolated from family and friends, almost held captive in their homes by deteriorating medical conditions. Some are confined to their bedrooms for much of the time with a lack of good weather and no family around them, sad and unhappy. The picture I see of "old" are those who've experienced bereavement, bad health, depression, not wanting to leave their home, and feeling they have no happy life to look forward to. Indeed, one of the key things they look forward to is the ring of the doorbell by the Meals On Wheels delivery person who has delivered their supply for the week, or perhaps their one hot meal of the day depending on what they can afford. I see another "old" person who once had a vibrant life either as a teacher, nurse or bus driver, confined to their home because of ill health and the ageing process compounded by bad weather, loneliness and isolation.

I am challenging my personal working experiences of "old" in the UK and want to turn this definition on its head via the Oxford dictionary. Let's implement another definition, or one to run alongside the medical realities, based on social experiences. I acknowledge that the ageing process is a universal issue and something which everyone will experience in different forms. No doubt I am sure there will be older people in Portugal equally confined to their homes by ill health and mobility problems. However, my other experiences of "old" within the charity I work for are "fun", "gusto", "determination", "attending the fitness club", "having a good time enjoying life despite the inevitable ageing process".

Indeed, what is natural ageing to someone over 55 is unnatural to another and we must recognize that the definition of old age in the Oxford Dictionary is not the only definition – I see other older people socializing, partying, having fun doing their hobbies with like-minded people of similar ages, such as travelling, keeping fit, dancing, and even dating. I recently attended a party hosted by Age UK Lambeth's MySocial service and wow! Was I blessed to experience firsthand "old" living "young". I saw people over 55 dressed up to the nines, looking colourful, wearing make-up, bright colours, and what my mum would have called "their Sunday best". It was an interaction of different cultures, backgrounds, sexes, ages – all coming together to have fun.

So what else can we do to challenge the standard dictionary definition of "old" applied to people in the UK? For those whose medical conditions prevent them leaving their home, we can bring the outside world into the lives of the lonely in the form of a volunteer companion. We can use the digital world via our phones or tablets to share music of their choice. We can have a personal agenda to ensure that every "old" person's home we go into, we do not leave without giving them hope and a vision that they can have a better life despite their problems. If the person is not totally confined to the home we can take them out for a walk, even if it is just around the block to a nearby garden or park.

We can listen to what they have to say. We can say positive words of encouragement and make them laugh. It is a medical fact that laughter and happiness promote longer life. Laughter Online University says, *"Laughing maintains a healthy endothelium and reduces the risk of cardiovascular disease, heart attack and stroke."*

We can connect them with other professionals who can help make their lives better by addressing other problems such as how to get a cleaner or shopping service, how to get bereavement support, how to get financial help if they have a very low pension or how to challenge an abnormally high electric or gas bill.

My experience is that "old" people have much to offer the world in terms of experience, value and enjoyment. Old is only as old as you feel; you can be a certain age on paper yet continue to have the vitality and determination to enjoy life even if you are hampered by mobility or medical issues. The concept of social networking services aimed at "older" people are crucial in promoting the "old to young" experience. Charity services aimed at tackling loneliness and isolation prove that people over 55 are not outdated or past the sell by date. Their work reduces the impact on medical service and shows that in the UK it is possible to make a difference. It just needs effort, passion, fun and a willingness to bring the outside world into an "older" person's home.

THE V PLAN DIET

Dominic Gugas

Do you know the hardest part of managing computer programmers – the thing that makes people compare it to herding cats? It's their personalities. I know, a lot of folks out there think that we programmers are drab little nerds with no personality at all, but in most cases, they simply could not be more wrong. Some programmers are pretty well-adjusted, like me. I can talk to people like an actual human being. My main failing is, if anything, being too willing to help, which is why I didn't turn them down when they offered me a role as team leader - all grief and no extra pay. Others, though... some other programmers have personalities like you would not believe. Personalities that would get them fired if they were burger flippers or interchangeable marketing drones. Personalities that make the prima donnas in Sales look calm and diplomatic. And personalities that sometimes just do not get along with each other. By which I mean, *spectacularly* do not get along.

Take Kirby and Holstein – two guys who used to be on my team. Both very good, each in their own way, at doing the job, and neither of them fit to be presented in any sort of company. Kirby was precise, methodical and neat. Anything he did, was done right. His code was meticulously commented, fully documented and adhered with every standard in the book, including the ones so obscure nobody else even knew they existed. It might take hours to get all the i's dotted and the t's crossed, but Kirby would put those hours in – not because he was paid for them (overtime had to be authorized three levels above a lowly team leader) but because, frankly, he would go completely bug-fuck nuts if he didn't. He had the sort of OCD that had to put the letters in the right order and call itself CDO.

Holstein was one of those annoying geniuses who never looks like he's doing any work. He could spend most of his day lounging at his desk, yakking about anything except the project we're working on, and then casually toss out an idea that saves the whole team two weeks' work and a million dollars in hardware spend. He easily rattled off the sort of stuff that just worked, first time, which was great even if I then spent so long kicking his ass to tell the rest of us how it worked so we could fix any problems that overall it took about as many days as giving it to Kirby would have done – which is to say, about half as long as anyone else would have taken, or about a quarter as long as the expensive contract resources would take to turn in stuff that didn't work at all.

They were total opposites in other ways too. Kirby was a health freak who lived on salads and bottled water. Holstein ate the sort of diet that would leave a student feeling ill. Kirby's desk was like his work – frankly, so neat and organized that he went past anally retentive and into Rain Man territory. Holstein was a slob whose crap overflowed onto the desks either side of his... one of which was Kirby's. There was a constant ebb and flow across the desks, a tide of food wrappers and comic book action figures that would surge across the dividing line only to be relentless pushed back to the border, but not one millimeter further.

Not entirely surprising that those two didn't get on anyway, but Holstein made things worse by being a practical joker of the worst kind. The most infamous example of which came when he noticed that Kirby had a regular routine of taking a potty break at a quarter to ten each morning and had a marked preference for trap number one in the facilities on our floor. So one particular morning Holstein nipped away from his desk at 9:40 and was back at 9:43 with an expression that sat the time I assumed was of relief, but was in fact a deep and abiding smugness. Three minutes after that, an anguished yell could be heard all across the floor. Trap one had been clingfilmed. Kirby's vengeance was swift and merciless. For the next two weeks all of the meetings that promised to be dull and interminable were booked to block out any opportunity Holstein might have had for lunch.

However, I guess the trouble really started the day Kirby lost his security pass. The tinpot Hitlers down in security held him until somebody could come to reception to sign him in. I was in the quarterly appraisal review, being told why none of my guys could be given a top performance rating – apparently you can't have one just because you've done a top-notch job, you need to 'evidence behaviours that live and excel the corporate values' - and for some reason Holstein didn't pick up my phone, so poor old Kirby spent nearly two hours cooling his heels. By the time I had escaped the meeting, picked up my voicemail and rescued Kirby, it was Holstein's favourite time of day – lunch. So, Kirby was pretty much in tears because all that time had been wasted and his day had deviated from The Plan and there Holstein was, sat at his desk with a large pizza (all the meats, plus anchovies) and one of his books on Paganism or Atlantis or something like that; he was always into weird stuff. The junk on Holstein's desk started with a Silicon Valley tarot deck and got progressively more bizarre from there. For Kirby, who was a zealously rational atheist in the Richard Dawkins mould, it was just one more annoying trait.

"I don't know how you eat – or read – that sort of crap," Kirby snarled as he sat at his desk and started unpacking and arranging his pens. Holstein made a few loud chewing noises and turned the page.

"Seriously, I do not know if your brain or your guts will rot first, the way you mistreat both!"

Holstein belched – a full, deep-throated roar that would do a lion proud. "Pardon," he said smugly. Kirby stood up and stomped off to the coffee machine, and when he came back, with what I devoutly hoped was decaf, he pointedly ignored Holstein.

I gave Holstein a warning glance. In fairness to him, while he could be an annoying, revolting S.O.B. he understood that there were limits, and that my "don't piss me off" stare meant that he had crossed them. He looked a bit sheepish, closed his pizza box and got back to work. That surprised me – not the working, but that there was still half a slice in the box. The only neat thing about Holstein is that he was always a "no food scrap left behind" kind of guy. If my glare could interfere with his appetite, it had to work even better than I thought it did. I'm not sure if the glare was a behaviour that excelled our corporate values – actually, I'm not convinced that 'excelling our values' is even good English – but if it was, I'd done it so well that my bonus was in the bag.

So, after having to give out everyone's disappointing appraisal, naturally we then went into crunch time – a couple of months of solid evenings and weekends working to meet our lords' and masters' utterly unachievable deadlines. Holstein pretty much lived on pizza and burgers at his desk, but never put on an ounce. Kirby was the one suffering – his skin became pale and mottled and his face puffy while his prized muscles lost their tone. Holstein naturally thought this was hilarious.

"Geez, are you putting on *more* weight? I thought your body was a temple."

"You can laugh - but I'll get back in shape once this project is done," Kirby snarled back. "You'll just get fatter as long as you keep eating junk. Heart disease, diabetes – you'll have to give up on chocolate or it'll kill you. No chocolate! And all of that processed meat is going to give you bowel cancer..."

"But it tastes so good! Yummy bacon, pepperoni pizza – sure you don't want to taste something that has, you know, actual taste, fat boy?"

"See how dying at fifty tastes, Holstein!"

"Dying at fifty?" Holstein grinned and started singing "I'm Mister Bad Example, take a look at me, I'll live to be a hundred and go down in infamy!"

"That's enough, Holstein," I sighed, giving him The Stare again. Fortunately, that still worked. The more we crunched, the more I had to stare, but the magic wasn't wearing out yet, thank God. "Lay off Kirby – we've all got too much work to do and enough troubles without creating more". I'm all for office banter, which in our world mostly consists of heartlessly persecuting your friends and co-workers, but you have to set limits, so things don't get out of hand. Kirby had already spoken to me about the strain the crunch working was causing him at home, and the last thing we needed right now was to make things worse for him. His wife, Carrie, had a good heart but she was as much of a perfectionist as her husband – probably why they made a couple. She was not impressed with the way he was gaining weight and had been 'encouraging' him to do something about it.

"I'll be OK," Kirby muttered, more to himself than to me. "Got a new diet plan – once this project is done, I'll double up on the gym time – it'll all be sorted out. It'll all be sorted out," he repeated.

When it became clear that the crunch wasn't going to end any time soon – which was when our dear leaders announced that we were moving to a 'new advanced working rhythm' that would 'shape the paradigm' for the industry', phrases that are apparently Harvard Business School-ese for 'work you dogs like galley slaves' – I shuffled the workloads around so Kirby could at least fit in a bit of gym time, and gave the expensive contractors something closer to their fair share of the workload. That earned me a colossal kicking for imperiling our good working relationship with trusted suppliers, and despite all that the dieting and the extra exercise were no help – in fact, it may have been overdoing both that led to Kirby's fatal heart attack. Carrie found him one morning, already cold, slumped across his rowing machine.

At the funeral, the dozen of us from the office outnumbered Kirby's bare handful of relatives and couple of friends who showed up. Maybe Holstein looked a little guilty at the funeral, but I think we all did. It was a shocking way to go, and the little funeral was a saddening and pathetic sight on such an inappropriately sunny summer's day.

Despite his song, Holstein didn't live to be a hundred. Less than two months later he was hit by a car while crossing the road outside our office to get his favourite lunch of a super-length chilli cheese dog from a food truck that was widely regarded as the best in the city. A man being killed in his early thirties is always a tragedy, but you know, in some ways I think it's the way he would have wanted to go. At the very least it was quick, and he died the way that he lived, reaching for something which would have been so good and yet so bad at the very same time. I guess that's as much as anyone can hope for, and Holstein did always say the death rate for couch potatoes was the same as for everyone else – one person, one death.

But here's the weird thing. When I went to clear out Holstein's desk, I found Kirby's missing security pass in there, its lanyard wrapped around a small doll, and the doll's mouth stuffed with pizza crumbs and desiccated hamburger. What does it mean? Well, I'm not as into the weird stuff as Holstein or as zealously rationalist as Kirby. I just don't know, but maybe there is a diet plan out there that really works.

THE MAN WHO NEVER SLEPT

Grahame Hood

It was the mildest Hogmanay night ever, both in terms of the weather and socially. Danny had invited me back to the seaside town where he came from with promises of the wildest parties I could wish for. Despite visiting all the pubs from about eight onwards, and meeting lots of people he knew, the elusive party invitations were not forthcoming. We found ourselves in The China Garden around eleven, where we did meet a girl who was a friend of a former girlfriend of mine. But again, no invite.

We saw the New Year in over a half bottle of Bells sitting on a rock looking out to sea. I was quite content to sit there for however long we felt like doing, and felt amazingly sober considering how much I had drunk.

Danny suddenly remembered somewhere we could go. "We'll go and see Rab, him and me used to go fishing a lot."

"Isn't it a bit late?"

"He'll be up. He never sleeps."

So we walked back into town through the council estate on the top of the cliff, and stopped at the door of what was probably the scruffiest house in the street. Sure enough there was a light on downstairs. Danny knocked on the door.

"Danny! How ya been? Come in the both o'yees!"

"Rab, this is Mark, the boy I share the flat with in Edinburgh"

I shook his hand, and we walked in to the downstairs lounge. The house was a wreck, bare floors and paper hanging off the walls. There was a three-seat sofa and two armchairs, one of which was occupied by a sleeping man.

"That's the wife's brother, the sanctimonious bastard. Drinks half my whisky and fa's asleep in ma chair. We'll have to keep it quiet, Sheila and the bairns are asleep upstairs."

I also saw a scruffy old collie dog fast asleep on a rug in front of the electric fire, snoring in synchronization with the sleeping brother in law. Rab fetched the remains of a bottle of whisky with glasses, and handed us each a can of Tennant's.

"It was good o'yees to come and see me, I don't get many visitors, I'm none too popular in this town as ye know, Danny."

"You were always good to me, taught me everything I knew about fishing, especially in the dark!"

"Well you know me, always the old night owl. I never get to bed much before dawn, and never sleep much when I do."

There was silence for a few minutes before I heard that a third snore had joined the rhythm; Danny was fast asleep too.

"So Mark, you share a flat with Danny? He's mentioned you. You play guitar, don't you? I used to play guitar. In Germany when I was in the Army in the sixties. I was pretty good too. Played in a wee band on the base and sometimes I'd go into town and play with the local guys in clubs. I had a good guitar too, a wee Hofner Club, you know the one? Two pickups, and a wee amplifier. You know Brian Jones, in the Stones? He was my hero, he could really play, classy guy. I wisnae like thae squaddies that live in Germany for three years and never bother learning any more German than they need to get a beer, or something tae eat. I even had a German girlfriend. She was a prostitute, but I didnae mind that. Her faither had a bar that I used to play in sometimes. She wanted to marry me. She'd have given it up for me, and we could have taken over the bar."

"Have you still got the guitar?"

"Naw, left it behind when I came back home."

"Why didn't you stay in Germany?"

"I'll tell you. One of my friends in the Army band, he wis the piano player, he could do you Jerry Lee Lewis, Little Richard, loved his rock and roll, but quiet, you know. Anyway, he got a Dear John letter. Seemed to take it pretty well, that sort of thing happens in the Army. You can't expect them to wait forever, and as ah said he was a quiet guy anyway. One night he set up a machine gun on a tripod in one of the huts, rigged it up with pulleys and wire so he could pull the trigger, and sat on a chair in front of it. I always wonder how long he sat looking at it before he pulled the wire. I wonder lots of things about how he must have felt, and what was going through his mind. Did he... Never mind. I was on guard duty that night and heard the shots and was first on the scene. Found the body. Nearly cut in half. Come, on I need some air."

We walked out through the kitchen into the garden. It was as untidy as the rest of the house. The sun had just risen, and we looked east along the Forth to the North Sea. It was incredibly quiet. I heard a slight noise behind me and turned to see Danny had woken up, and was standing at the kitchen door rubbing his eyes.

"C'mon Mark, it's about time we went home."

Rab yawned and said he was off to bed too.

We all walked back through the house (the brother in law and collie still snoring in perfect harmony) and said goodbye on the front doorstep. Rab went back inside and we continued down the street.

"Where are we going now Danny?"

"We'll go back to my folk's house, maybe get a bit of breakfast."

"Rab was telling me about his time in the Army, in Germany."

"He's never really told me about that. He was born here and joined the Army quite young. Then he came back when he left and got married and had a couple of kids. Never seemed to settle though. Could never hold a job for long. A lot of the local people think he's just a waster, a scrounger. But he's been a good friend to me."

"Yeah, he said."

"Never used to talk about his time in the army though. I expect he had a good time in Germany in those days."

"Yeah, he told me all about it. He had a great time"

THE LAUGHING EUNUCH

Cleo Felstead

No one had dared laugh in Wan Li's court for over 200 years. Emperor Wan Li's great grandfather had banned it 207 winters ago after falling flat on his face at a great ball.

The only laughter heard since that time had come from an innocent young servant who let out a tiny snigger on hearing Emperor Wan Li's wife belch at the dinner table. Wan Li was outraged and immediately sent him to be fed to his pet dragons, Gong Gong and Chi Chi. The Emperor, in his wisdom, felt that his wife was also an embarrassment and fed her to his pet leopards Chobi and Kai.

Let me introduce myself. My name is Lui Jin, Emperor Wan Li's head eunuch. I have written this story to share with you my masters rather spectacular fall from grace. Unlike many fellows in my profession I read and write very well but don't tell, as the court would have my head for treachery. So shhh! Keep this a secret, please.

The morning of his down fall was, at first, following its normal routine. The normal routine mainly revolving around filling up Wan Li's huge stomach. Flocks of cooked pheasants and platters of wolf meat we consumed in a blink of an eye, all of which seemed to hardly touch his rather bulgy sides. He just kept eating. But what happened next on this particular morning was an unexpected delight. The Emperor, on trying to stand from his chair, found that his big fat bottom had wedged itself firmly into his grand throne.

Let me tell you, this man's backside was bigger than the eastern sector of the Great Wall and he consumed more food in a day than his pet boars ate six seasons through.

I have to say, he had ignored the warning signs. The horizon of his waistline had been extending beyond the vestige of his golden throne for a good few months now. All those yellow bird buns and crab dinners had taken rise in him. His waist's expansion had been a rapid affair ever since he could not find a replacement wife. He'd been eating six feasts a day for months now.

I had tried to mention it during his bath time but after receiving a threat worse than castration I decided to let the Emperor's waistline determine its own position in the world.

His servants tried to get him out; pulling, pushing, yanking, greasing but nothing worked.

As I was standing at the bottom of the velvet steps, watching his face simmer to purple with frustration, something took a hold of me. I suddenly found it all so incredibly funny.

'You will be fed to the dragons!' I warned myself, but as much as I knew my life depended on not doing so, I desperately, desperately wanted to laugh.

The Emperor was straining so hard to get out some air escaped from his behind. That was it. I could restrain myself no longer. I did it. It flew out of me like a rampaging warrior. I started laughing so loudly I'm sure the tremors were felt in Timbuktu.

The room fell to a deathly silence around me. The emperor stopped.

'What was that sound?' boomed the Emperor from the top of the steps.

I froze, slaughter vivid in my mind's eye.

'What was that sound?' he repeated.

Silence. The ancient law had been broken. He looked straight at me.

My palms began to sweat, and I stood paralyzed. The Emperor tried to stand. I went to run, but before I could, something wonderful happened. Wan Li's throne rocked onto its two front legs, toppled forwards and fell down the velvet steps. He landed with a humongous splat face first on to the marble floor below. A stifled groaning could just about be heard from under the throne.

Everyone in the room stayed still, stunned by the sight. That was until a noise from quite far behind me landed on my ears. A servant at the back of the hall was stifling a laugh. All eyes stayed forward but unable to resist this freedom, one by one, the whole room sprung to life with sniggers. Before we knew it the court had erupted into a raucous choir of laughter. It was beautiful.

'Get me out of here,' the Emperor's muffled voice called through the laughing.

Now listen, I don't remember who took the first step or if anyone said anything or formulated a plan, but get him out, we did. Do you know what the 200-strong court did after our laughter had subsided? We picked the emperor up, chair and all, carried him outside, opened the cage to his dragons and pushed him in. It took several days but the Emperor was never seen again.

A great party was thrown, and everyone laughed and laughed and laughed. Hours of laughing bounced off the palace walls until everyone's bellies ached and they all got a little bit hungry. A feast was had, and all Wan Li's food came to good use, people ate nonstop for days. It was the most joyous of times. 200 years of forbidden laughter set free.

It wasn't long before Wan Li's ruthless cousin Yongle Chong galloped in and took control. Our laughter and feasting stopped, and a few heads were lost.

However, once a year, when Chong is in his deep snoring slumber, we all secretly gather in that great hall to remember Wan Li's great fall from grace. We take turns to sit on the throne where Wan Li once sat and reenact his plight, laughing until our sides split in two. We call it the festival of 'Wobbly Wan Li' and when the laughing is done, we all go back to our work knowing deep in our hearts that short shadows give way to long ones and that the tiger will always follow the ox.

BEAUTIFUL AND BRUTAL

Jeannine Lehman

My English friends always want to know about American football, and how it is 'real sport' with all the padding, and how it can be enjoyed with all the stopping and starting and the hundreds of rules that seem to make no sense. And admittedly, I have a hard time explaining to Non-Believers how this game is both brutal and beautiful. But it is.

I grew up with American football; my father played at both University and professional level, and was a football coach my whole life. He taught me how to throw when I was 5 years old, and I learned the rules from that point. I went with him on Saturday mornings for scrimmages, and throughout my childhood and teenage years I went with him to scout other teams. That's when the beauty of the game began to make sense. I was able to see things on the field, and began to understand the strategies necessary to play tough and to win. Those times are when I also began to absorb the lessons on mental and physical toughness that my father wanted to teach me, so that life would never beat me down.

I was the oldest of two girls, a fact my father never mentioned as significant, but must have been. In an age when women's rights were just becoming prevalent he must have been one of the Midwest's first truly enlightened men as he simply forgot my gender and got on with teaching me how to play every sport, how to compete, how to win, and how to play even when hurt. He taught me football at a level that most boys would kill for. And I was good.

I grew up, I continued to play in Uni and after. There were always leagues for any group of people who wished to play a sport, that's American culture for you. We love to encourage competitiveness. And the game of American football continued to grow and thrive, becoming a very large part of the culture. There is a feeling in the air during Autumn as families gather on weekends to watch games, sometimes traveling miles to see a favourite team. But I dwell too much on the beautiful side.

The dark side is the brutality of American football. It is a sport that although players wear pads, the ethos of the game is pain. We know now, of course, that the concussions, subsequent brain damage and other maiming side effects are the inevitable outcome of years of abuse on the field.

And yet that doesn't reduce the enthusiasm of players and fans. An odd thing there. I'm sure you will agree with me - I will say it one more time, just so it's clear - the ethos of the game is pain. You must be willing to rush headlong into it, play with it, cause it to happen to others, and finally celebrate the pain of the game.

When I moved to Chicago, I joined a league with 10,000 American football players. We played on teams, in leagues similar to the way English football is set up. At the same time, I began my first real job as a derivatives trader. I'm sure it is not much of a surprise given my upbringing that my job was almost entirely dominated by men, yet there I was. My Father was so proud, but I had an inkling he was far more interested in my weekend football than in my career as a trader. Nevertheless, as I dutifully phoned my parents every Sunday he would talk me through the week's ups and downs, always, always prodding me to be tough.

After a year in the regular Chicago league, I was recruited to play football in the elite league. This was an invitation-only league mostly comprised of guys who played in University and were now working instead of playing pro. The teams were co-ed, meaning women and men played together, and although the rules stipulated touch football only, it was always nearly full contact. My Father was thrilled.

I frequently played quarterback as it was truly unusual to have a girl who could not only throw, but throw accurately, and hit a receiver going at full speed from 40 yards. But the level of contact as a quarterback is intense. At first, the opposite linemen (usually 6'5" ish, 17/18 stone) would be somewhat amused at a girl (and small girl at that – 5'4", 9 stone) running the offense of the team. But then the frustration would set in, the amusement would die, and the tackling would commence.

The second week in, I phoned on Sunday and we began the weekly format; a recitation of all the injuries I was playing with, how to treat them effectively, and most importantly, how to continue to play hurt. That week was a sprained wrist, a cleated calf, and a bruised tail bone. Believe me, the list of injuries just grew each week as the other teams faced down their frustration and just let it flow all over me when they breached the protection of my offensive line. In a weird, parallel way, it was my first year on a trading floor, which can also be a beautiful, brutal place, so those Sunday talks also helped buoy me for the verbal abuse and constant challenge of that live-and-die atmosphere.

But the beautiful side of the game is just as sharp when you are marching down the field, calling plays that bring out the best in your receivers who are lightning fast, or perhaps making surprise calls that leave the other team confounded. And Dad always wanted to hear about those as well.

Halfway through the season, the Sunday call involved almost-healed bruised ribs, a sprained ankle that had bothered me since high school and was injured again, and a very sore left side from taking a hit from a guy twice my size. The conversation started with work and how I was doing, but I could tell Dad wanted to speak about football. I had managed to score a couple of touchdowns the day before which he was dwelling on while lecturing me on the toughness required to get back out there next week. I was annoyed with him and having a tough time with the beauty, as the brutality was all my bruised body could think about. But as I told you before – the ethos of the game is pain. You must be willing to rush headlong into it, play with it, cause it to happen to others, and finally celebrate the pain of the game. I had known this almost from birth and would deal with it the following week.

I had to. My father died suddenly the next day.

FOUR THEMES ON SUMMER

Simon Thompson

Floating in a shallow pool by a Cornish beach. Earlier that day I got lost in the hotel's corridors and scared my parents. As a result, I have been allowed a big ice cream with two scoops: one chocolate and the other mint. Naturally. I plan to get lost more often. Mummy and Daddy smell funny. I now know this to be gin but back then it was unfamiliar; a sharp citrus scent as Mummy pressed my chocolatey face against hers. I'm looking up at the blue sky and listening to the sounds of other children playing. I think I want to be four forever.

Sitting beside the pool in the crazy, bleaching sunlight of the Cote d'Azure. In my hands, dog-eared and spine broken, is a paperback copy of the Odyssey. I've been trying to read this since six am, but the Greek is swimming in front of my eyes. I daren't stop though, as I made such a point of it the evening before, getting into a prolonged and pointless argument with Father about how I was going to do something interesting with my life, unlike him. Lloyd Cole and his pretentious, jangly guitar pop are playing through the headphones of my Walkman. It's 1990 and more than anything I want my life to race forward.

In the middle of a triangle on the sand made by a South African, a Kiwi and me, sits a shortwave radio. Two thousand miles south by southwest from me is Ellis Park, and the Springboks are playing the All Blacks in the Rugby World Cup final. The signal fades in and out which is driving us mad. As the match goes into overtime the sun is setting over the island of Zanzibar, and we are opening new beers. This is no easy task without an opener, but the South African has a way of doing it. He doesn't want to open the Kiwi's beer. The two teams are caught in a stalemate. As the sky darkens and the humidity rises, that incomparable fly half, Joel

Stransky, kicks a drop goal and one of us cheers. I've left university and am clueless to my future.

A beautiful blonde takes my hand and walks me to the side of the pool. Christ, it's hot today in Cyprus. It's 36 degrees in the shade as I stroll over alongside her, breathing in the wild thyme which grows in the cracks of the stony hills where we are staying. I watch her as she dives in, leaving only a tiny splash as she does so. She swims a length underwater, and I hear the television in the villa. Yet more Brexit deadlock and I'm not interested. As her head emerges from the water she turns back to me, blue eyes flashing, and says, "Daddy, are you coming in now?" I want this moment to stay forever.

TRUTH

Siobhan Reardon

"You should know, a million-pound deal is riding on this". He was at her elbow, breathing down into her face. His face was well cooked and red, his cuffs snow white, and the swell of him, so close, his cologne coming over her in lemony-sugar drifts. Like too much cake.

Mr. Greaves. One of the partners. One of the people who were waiting for her, the chief librarian, to get her facts right. It was a matter of moments – her at her desk, sitting with stillness and certainty, printing off a document that she would hand to him while time slowed and waited, and tension underscored every breath.

The light stole in through the library windows in slow-yellow. They were positioned on the ground floor, next to the facilities department and the post room – a big clue to their status. She returned to her office every day at ten from the morning meeting on the top floor, and every day she took a deep breath, as the lift doors closed on her and plummeted. She willed herself not to panic. Suspended in glass, she fell to earth. The office went by with a mechanical gleam, and a brief glimpse of other levels, desks and faces, all in soft focus, and frondy plants creeping sickeningly around chrome -the only bright things there, a noxious lurid green. Her face flamed red, a bleak wounding blast of vertigo, before the lift doors finally opened and she felt the air again, and the shiny corridor beneath her feet.

Tap-tap-tap, her heels went discreetly along its polished surface. And every day she went through it - her fear of falling become routine- but she wouldn't let herself take the staircase. She tasted her terrors and she bit down on them.

They knew nothing of this, the Greaves's in their ice castle. They knew only this – certainty. Relief. A deal clinched. A whirr of printed document. She handed it to him primly, as a marker of her annoyance. All faces in the room turned towards her. He scanned the document for the relevant passage. And with hardly a word broke away through the thick library doors, swinging bulkily, merrily, towards the lifts with the lemon-sugar coating of his success at his coat tails. He was unique in his awfulness. Dickensian in his proportions. He had no kindness, no thanks, no compunction.

But at her back her staff of seven, smiling.

They would celebrate later. And she would come through the front door tonight to her little boy, carrying a big basket of fruit, which would have arrived on her desk with a note from the chief partner's secretary: "With thanks."

For all this awfulness she earned so much more than she ever would have dreamt of as a student in the downbeat halls where she had once hovered – hoping always for more handing in her assessments, climbing a ladder that with her every breath she willed herself up. It made her cold, all that hoping.

Voicing opinions in class, talking up, always talking up, volunteering, "very helpful", very "observant", "very focused" her tutors said, as hands folded in her lap and she allowed herself a small smile.

Like the awful Mr. Greaves, she had her own classic scent – but it was the plume of pure cold air. Cold fingers turning pages, quick wrists holding books to her chest, having them out of the library weeks before anyone else, a week ahead, a step ahead, already a world away – and never really that well liked for it.

*

"Beauty is truth, Truth Beauty" she found printed on a postcard in her locker one day. She looked around the corridor and saw nothing but bare linoleum. Nobody coming. No smiling lanky guy ready to step forth and speak. And there were no clues as to who would write her a love letter. Well, it wasn't a love letter exactly; it was the topic for the week's discussion in her literary criticism class. But it was now relevant to her. She smiled to herself, she hummed, and went back to her room and plucked her eyebrows and rubbed cocoa butter on her knees and elbows.

And then the next day he was there, beside her in the library while she tried to focus on her study. Someone from that same class. Talking when he knew he shouldn't – shifting her outside with a big smile and a promise that he'd "shut up if she came for coffee". And so it came - coffee and Kudos.

Her standing in the eyes of others increased overnight by two hundred times. And he never left.

He made it so easy for her. Jon. Jaunty, relaxed and easeful. Good to be with. He wasn't clever, but he had a real gift, and that gift was being himself. He even said of himself that he "would always get by". And he would. For he was that rare and wonderful thing, a happy man. And he became hers –at her side, in her bed – and next to her brittleness he was soft as toffee. So sweet and so warm-smelling that her joy in the mornings when she woke beside him came over her like grief.

On a Spring morning when the light hitting the windows of the big shops on Piccadilly came along in waves like camera flashes, shocking people out of their lethargy, and the air smelt green and good even in the city, and women walked by smartly, hitching their handbags higher on their shoulders and sweeping their faces upwards in a little luxuriant tilt, and gangs of young boys of indeterminate age stumbled along in groups in a state of hormonal fustiness – startled like fox cubs, their badly dyed hair sticking up at odd angles, their stick thin elbows pushing out of soft cloth shirts –Grace moved along with her six year old son, firmly holding his hand. "Now don't let go!" she had warned him before they left home, which made him feel so anxious that at one point he squeezed her palm so tight she cried "Ouch!" and snatched it back. But they were happy. It was the weekend, and they were going to see Daddy in the bookshop and to take him out to lunch. He worked half days on Saturdays and this was their routine. He also picked Owen up from school most days, and he had told him once when he met him at the school gates that he was "a part time worker and a full time Dad". When Owen asked: "So what is Mum then?" the reply came with a smile. "Son, your Mum is an enigma." But Owen couldn't say that strange word and he soon forgot about it.

The bookshop was big. There were three floors, and lots of staff and a café in the basement. It was bright and airy and had a good buzz. Grace cast about for him. She could feel Fiona staring over in their direction from the counter where she was serving and tried very hard to not catch her eye. Fiona: Quick, efficient, rounded. Opinionated, ponytailed and completely charmless with the customers. Her hair was pulled back so tight it must have hurt, and she kept a glue eye on everything. She was of course brilliant at her job and she had been there for years. She was loyal to Jon to the point of over-possessiveness, placing herself so firmly at the center of their little family that they could at times only look on a little mesmerized and more than a little embarrassed by her mistake. "And how's the wee little man?" she would call in her strong Glaswegian accent, her face lighting up in delight like a fond Aunty, dishing out presents and wisdom. Grace had seen Fiona in action so many times; her possessiveness of Jon and her soft bullying. Blocking a call, bouncing a hanger on or some poor student looking for work, with the words, "I told him you were way too busy right now . . ." delivered to Jon with a knowing smile and a brief downward glance of complicity. Grace sometimes watched as he played up to it, grinning, and surrendered his powers as a ploy. "Oh, just go and ask Fiona . . ." delivered within earshot, and "Fife, I would be lost without you." Fiona drank it all up like a kitten drinking milk. It was quite ruthless. But he needed things to work. His charm was a heavy blanket, and it gave a warmth from which they all benefitted. This was the truth, and however queasy Grace felt about it she had to find a way to accept it. It's not the big questions, she sometimes thinks, late at night – the questions of love and sex and kids – but the small things that really hit you, like when the man you love is sometimes just a bit of a user. When did that creep in? Or that young guy that you first kissed and loved – well, he's a lot more flinty lately and why is that? She couldn't allow herself to think about it, she shut her eyes and she shut it out and sleep came on her like a dropped curtain.

"What's up son!" Jon would say, swinging Owen into the air, in their little Saturday routine, catching him from behind the bookcases where he was darting, pretending to hide: "Think I didn't see you!" And the child's laughter rang out and there were smiles and pauses and customers looked up from their browsing to watch their family exit the shop, the three of them in complete tandem, the child in the middle and the parents looking straight ahead, ceremoniously, holding a little hand each, and only a little smug at their own happiness and how it rubbed off on others.

But today, on this spring morning the little man was darting, and his Dad wasn't looking. He came closer and closer to where his Father stood, running in little concentric circles, and giggling, but Jon was immersed in a conversation and seemed oblivious to them both. He was talking to a woman. Her back was to them and Grace had an impression of very small shoulders and short dark hair. They were bantering – arguing and laughing. "Listen, you don't get ahead of yourself now, I'm still your boss, so get back to work, immediately!" For some reason they both seem to find this hilarious. Grace feels a wave of annoyance at Jon's insensitivity and a stab of hurt for little Owen. He has by now stopped running and is looking back at his Mother over his shoulder, his eyes uncertain and the start of a tremor in his lower lip.

Grace steps up. She taps Jon sharply on the shoulder and himself and the girl spring back. She is very pretty, with a fine boned freckled face and wide set brown eyes. On seeing her the girl freezes. Jon just looks shocked. "Hallo I'm Grace, Jon's wife. And this little man is Owen, and we've come to take this man to lunch," and she leans up and kisses him on the cheek. Job done.

But the girl makes a quick recovery, smiles and offers her hand so that Grace has no choice but to return the handshake. "Grace hi, I'm Naomi and it's great to finally meet you. I've heard loads about you both." She drops Grace's hand and looks down at Owen as he grins and climbs up into his Father's arms, placed at the center of things and happy once again. The two women regard each other. Grace sees the girl's vanity - her tight body, the taut hint of shoulder strap, the slim fit jeans looped with a fine leather belt held by a turquoise stone at the center. She sees her good skin and the gloss in her hair, and the gleaming silver rings on her fine boned fingers. She sees what her husband sees when he looks at her, and she doesn't like it. "Actually, Grace (Stop saying my name she wants to shout at her! Who are you anyway, I don't even know you!) we were just talking about the book launch that's coming up in a couple of weeks. Y' know the big launch? Oh, I really hope that you can make it! It's taken a lot of organizing but we've got some good new authors lined up and it's going to be brilliant! And this man," she says, gesturing to Jon, "is also going to be reading some of his own work which we're all very excited about.

He's so talented". Grace looks at Jon. Jon looks down at the floor. He hadn't told her anything about the book launch. And she sees a ghost of a grin crossing the girls' face. She is having fun with her, and with a mockery so explicit and light that it's plain she isn't afraid of her. Grace realises with a jolt that what she has just heard between her husband and this awful girl is the warm fizz of sexual attraction. The sudden knowledge floors her. Not in a million years would she have she ever seen that coming! She looks on, stunned by her own humiliation.

"So, anyway you folks, see you all later. I have to go now and relieve Fiona." She pulls a face and walks away with head aloft, so brimful with bodily awareness that heads turn as she strides on with her long neck and that lightness in her step that speaks of confidence and purpose and management skills. And all Grace can think of to say is "How long exactly has she been working here?"

He looks towards the door as if he wants to make a run for it. "Three weeks."

*

And so it sits between them like a stiffness in the spine, that girl shaped thing that has come into their home. They don't talk about it. But like a giant amoeba it moves and fuses and occupies space. The silences that descend are awful. But Grace refuses to challenge him. She will not speak of it. And no, she tells herself, she doesn't believe that Jon would actually sleep with that girl, but the point is that he wants to – so is there really much difference? Her heart hurts. She has lost the luxury of trust. His behaviour is now an odd mix of embarrassment and overcompensation, followed by complete abstraction as if a switch were thrown and he simply wasn't there. She catches him staring in the bathroom mirror for long moments at a time. He can't always look her in the eye. And they don't touch. Instead they act out a version of normal life, waking in the morning to little fat palms of light touching the double-glazed windows, oozing like olive oil, and the duvets thrown off, and breakfast TV on and the child running between them, one to the other, shouting "Weetabix! I want Weetabix!" as his Daddy tries to hold him down long enough to get him dressed for school and his Mum picks up her big soft handbag and her keys and moves towards the front door.

Work: All around her people twitter. Men's voices boom. In the white spaces of the work café strident women flick their wrists to shake sweetener into their coffee whilst they chatter on their mobile phones, sitting only with the other partners and never with their secretaries. In this place where admin staff are still referred to as secretaries, like something out of the 1960's, everyone is in their separate groups and they stay that way. Grace makes a point of sitting with her own team while she eats chicken salad, reading her book while they gossip and chatter. And sometimes she catches herself thinking as she glances up at them that she wishes she knew how to make friends. She just never had the knack.

On the night of the reading she is at home alone. Things hit a new ice plateau when he asks on his way out, "Will you come tonight Grace?" His eyes are steady. "Won't you come? Please come. I asked Anna and we can still get her to babysit." He is standing above her at the kitchen table as she sits drinking coffee, and he looks formal and courteous, body slightly bent forward, good shirt pressed, a spritz of aftershave and a question on his lips - stepping up with his old-world charm as if he were an admirer asking her for the first dance. She wants to spit flames. She who had never flirted, never looked at other men, never wanted anyone but him. If hoping so hard had once made her cold, rage now shot through her with a bright burn, making two round spots simmer in her cheeks and giving her eyes a watery shine. And in that moment, she hated him for making her into that woman. The wife: pert, possessive, a walking cliché, pulling rank amongst a nest of gossips and a young woman who only laughed at her. She turns her face to profile and won't even reply.

He walks to the door and pauses, a heaviness in the set of his shoulders, and turns back to her. "Grace, y'know something? You are smarter than me and we both know it. You are smart as a whip. You can do anything you set your mind to and always have, you are a force of nature, and sometimes to be honest you frighten me a little. And yes, you do everything for me and the little man and we love you for it, but I have to tell you something now and I should have said it a long time ago." He raises an arm and points, a flash of temper in his eyes. "The thing about you Gracie is that you've just got no give. None. Never have. Never will. And I really don't want Owen to end up like that."

And the door slams on her astonishment.

He didn't come home that night. She drank large glasses of chilled white wine as if it were water and temper and doubt and fear crashed through her in great gusts. And she wept. In her bed in the early hours, splayed out, the room spinning, she felt the wheel of memory rearing up on her in all it's sad, sick colour, there she was falling to earth in the lift, there he is stooping to lace up his shoes tightly. There she is in bed with him the first time, in her little dormer room all spangly with light. There's him laughing at things she could never find funny, he'd always have to explain the joke and eventually just give up, head in hands. There it is, her baby belly. And the brilliant whiteness of dawn on the morning Owen was born. Cold Christmas lights strung along the Embankment and fear unfurling in her as they drove home. Motherhood; would she get it right?

There are his new shoes wheeled back again into view in dizzying clarity – the colour of the blue stitching around the edges and the soft burnished shine of them, fresh as newly fallen conkers. Soft. Expensive. She found them hidden under the bed amongst rills of dust, still in the box, as if he were ashamed of spending so much on himself, or of her knowing how much they cost. And there he is exactly as he will be tonight, in the room, wearing them, a generous full-hearted man coaxing nervous young writers forward with a hand on the shoulder, a hearty congratulation at their success and little rueful aside. "And he used to work here! Never saw that one coming." They would all laugh. There he stood smiling, laughing, spinning his yarns, a colossus with a well-trimmed beard, and that beautiful voice that carried so much authority and moved anyone who heard it. He was the warm up act. He was The Bard. He was a little bit of both, and they all loved him for it.

"Writers - I'm sick of them." In the cool decaying dawn her eyes shuttered with half-light and a pain glancing in her temples she hears these words. She jolts awake, confused, and sees the shape of him standing over by the window and the shout of "Where were you?" doesn't even leave her lips. She is afraid. It is obvious that he is distressed and that he is also still drunk. The room floods with the stink of stale alcohol and bad food and bile backs up in her throat as she sits up in the bed with the covers drawn around her. He sways heavily on his feet and as if it were the most natural thing continues with his monologue. "They're all writers, the whole bloody lot of them, it's like a zombie movie in there. I can't move for them! And then they act like agony Aunties and give advice and hoover up each other's nasty little secrets, and then they write about them. Bastards."

And he stops and whispers. "And I'm never going to be one of them."

That silence then – such a big silence.

He gives her a look so piercing that she has to look away. She sees it now – what she had never wanted to acknowledge. Those little sighs and asides amongst the staff, eyes shifting, and young trendy guys standing in a row with their arms folded tight across their chests truculently. A captive audience. And those smirks. And all this time he was oblivious. "He's not reading his own stuff again tonight, is he? Oh, no." Did she overhear that? Did someone say that – when? She aches for him, for all the days of rota's and arrangements and the school run, all the many compromises that he made just to survive, all that frittering away of a talent that he simply didn't possess.

He goes silent after saying this and then abruptly he crashes and hits the floor. He groans. She doesn't touch him, she just leaves him as he curls up in a tight ball and falls into a dead sleep. Then she lays a blanket over him, places a washing up bowl next to his head and unfurls the document rolled up in his hand. She goes back to the kitchen, takes two paracetamols with a big glass of water, sits down at the table and starts to read.

She had carved them up. The girl. Naomi. Brazenly and in print for everyone to see. She wrote about all of them, not just him. There they were in technicolor and easily identifiable - the whole three floors. Their jostling and in-fighting, their little cliques and their love affairs -who was the loudmouthed one who everyone hated, who stole things from the fridge, who always smelt of garlic and who looked up women's skirts as they walked up the stairs. Who only dressed in black. Who cried easily and so could never be criticized. It went on and on, with vivid descriptions and with only the names changed, and the books were a mere backdrop to the drama. The descriptions of the public were just as unforgiving, but the descriptions of Fiona made her gasp. She had really nailed her. A cartoon character, a bully, a sergeant major with a soft spot for kids. Grace could almost hear Fiona's voice rising from the page. Jon in contrast was a lightweight - too nice, too idle, letting Fiona do all the work and obsessed by his wife and child. She winced at the passage where he shows 'photos of them to people who haven't asked, producing his mobile cheerily from his pocket. "Here, have a look at this." When she gets to the part where he reads aloud to his captive audience she stops. It's just too much for body and soul to take.

Morning finally blooms. It staggers in on wispy trails of light and a low hum of traffic. She opens the windows of their room to let the fresh air in, stepping over him to reach the sill. Never has she been so happy that the night was over. She lies down beside him on the carpet and curls into him. His stubble grates her cheek with a not unpleasant buzz and he cups his hand to her head. Ripples of drink radiate over her, but she doesn't care. She feels his physical warmth like a longing. Like before.

She knows he's awake without him even moving.

"I take it she's gone?"

"Yes. She left that present for us. It's already been published. So I s'pose that's my job gone then."

"Why would she do such a thing?"

"I don't really know. Maybe just because she could."

"Grace," he starts.

She puts a finger to his lips. "No, don't say it. Don't break the spell, please."

They lie in a rough tumble. Her stomach groans for tea and toast but she doesn't want to move.

"We stink by the way."

"I know, but you stink more than me."

He laughs. He hugs her to him.

"Jon I'm sorry."

"It's okay."

"It's just so hard. I try so hard. And I know that whatever I do nobody ever likes me the way they like you. People love you, they really love you."

"Now it's your turn to not say another word. Just leave it go my little enigma."

She breathes in.

"I'll tell you a secret," he says thoughtfully.

"What?"

"The truth is we're all a mess - a great big bloody mess! And we're all just trying. And that's what makes us human. And that's okay."

"And I'll tell you something else."

"What?"

"You. Skittering down the corridors at Uni, in your little kitten heels and your nose in the air, repelling all boarders. Beautiful."

"You remember that?"

"Of course I do".

He curls his hand around her wrist in a movement so delicate she almost can't bear it.

"So what now?" she asks rotating her wrist in his palm.

"You mean what are we going to do with ourselves?"

"Yes".

"You mean what's the plan?"

"Yes"

"Well first we're going to set our son a really good example and ring in sick, then have breakfast and afterwards take him to the park and throw bread at the ducks."

"And after that?"

"After that I really have no idea."

BAD MAN

Robert Williams

I was washing some dishes when it happened. The water was so hot I could only just put my hands in it, yet I could still feel goose pimples rising on my arms. It felt like a cold wind had blown through the kitchen but, on a hot still day in July, there was no such thing as a cold wind and that meant only one thing. A ghost had come to visit.

It's one of the things that happen when you're an urban witch. A sort of occupational hazard. Witches of all types attract ghosts, but urban witches attract more. London has been rumoured to have more ghosts than living people, and a few of them occasionally make their way to my flat on the 16th floor of Talltree Towers.

I put the kettle on and sat down to wait for it to boil. That gave me time to put myself in the right frame of mind to receive a ghost. My rural colleagues that go in for the dark clothing and dancing around naked before dawn would say they were opening themselves to the psychic plane, but I prefer to think of it as just relaxing. It had been a busy day after all. I'd had three séances and a tarot reading, and I'd seen to poor Mr Atkins, bedridden on the fifth floor. That nurse didn't come out to him often enough for my liking.

It was all bread-and-butter work and, although nothing in the day had been that taxing, taken as a whole, it had been pretty draining. I had hoped to put my feet up with a large gin and to make a significant dent in my boxed set of *Downton*. My visitor changed all that.

When the kettle boiled, I made tea. It was a bag-in-a-cup job. I preferred a pot of loose leaf but felt lazy, and it was only for me, after all. I didn't think my visitor would either want or even be capable of drinking one.

I took a sip and, sufficiently calmed, started to speak.

"What do you want, love?" I asked in my gentlest voice. I wasn't expecting an answer. Ghosts are surprised when anyone takes notice of them and it takes them a little while to realise they are being addressed.

I gave it a minute then spoke again. "My name's Mags, love. I'm a witch. I can hear you if you want to talk to me."

"I killed him." I barely heard her. She wasn't used to talking.

"Killed who, dear?"

Well, there was no need to guess what she wanted. The guilty ones always wanted absolution. It didn't matter who gave it. Confession is good for the soul, especially when you're dead.

"I killed him." She was louder and stronger but was fixated on her message. The vaguest of shadows was starting to form in front of my cooker.

"Who, dear? Who did you kill?"

I sometimes worry my professional voice makes me sound like Claire Rayner.

"Bad man."

I sighed. This was going to take a while. I eyed the boxed set of Downton and knew I wouldn't be watching any of it tonight.

"Who is the bad man, love?"

"Husband. Bad man." I sighed.

"Why was he bad? Did he hit you?"

She was silent for a long time. I thought maybe she'd gone but the room hadn't warmed up and the shadow was still there.

"I don't remember," she said at last.

Ghosts tended to lose track easily. I've heard other witches call it the death trauma. From what I've heard, death seems a bit like changing gear without a clutch while wearing a blindfold. I guess it makes you forget a few things.

The shadow now had the vague shape of a woman. I directed my words toward her.

"When did it happen? When did you kill him?"

"Just now."

I cursed myself for being stupid. Spirits have no sense of time. It was always just now to them. It could literally have been just now, or it could have been decades ago.

The shadow had gained a little more substance. I could see the definite outline of a woman, and she was wearing a dress of some sort. It could have been a coat. It was difficult to tell. There was still no colour or texture to her.

I was getting nowhere so I decided to try a different tack.

"Why have you come to see me, love?"

"I don't know." There was a pause before she spoke.

My main-and-only theory was still that she wanted to be forgiven. She'd killed her husband after he'd hit her one too many times. I'd seen it so often on the estate, although generally the wife was still alive.

"It's not your fault, you know. You were only defending yourself."

"Bad man."

That confirmed it. He'd been hurting her, and she lashed out in self-defence.

"Yes, dear. Bad man. What did he do?"

She was silent.

"Did he hurt you, dear?"

"Yes. Hurt. He hurt me."

"Did he hit you?"

"No."

I sighed. She was really the most difficult woman.

"You need to tell me a little more before I can help you, dear. You do want my help, don't you?"

"I don't know."

Curious. Why else would she be here? I decided to take a gamble.

"How did you die, dear?"

Often ghosts have no idea they have died. The truth was sometimes hard to handle.

"I ...," she hesitated. Perhaps I had gone too far after all. "I fell. Stairs. Railing. I was running."

She probably died here in the block. Spirits rarely wander far and quite a few people have met their end on the stairs in this block. The crap lighting, the worn steps, the low railings. It was a recipe for disaster.

"Why were you running?"

I thought of all the deaths on the stairs I could remember in the years since I moved into this block. The old woman who tried to escape a mugger but didn't spot the skateboard. The little girl running from a fire. The man who'd stayed a little too long at the pub and was late for his dinner.

None of them matched the shadow slowly taking form in front of me or the voice of the middle-aged woman I could hear. By now, she appeared pretty much solid although she still had no colour. She was a moving obsidian statue that somehow felt familiar. I couldn't put a name to her though. She was a woman I knew but not well enough and her features were triggering a memory that tickled at the back of my mind. The lack of colour didn't help.

"I needed to see you."

She was coming to see me? Running?

"Were you coming for my help, dear?"

She wouldn't have been the first person to come running to me. Urban witches are known, by some, as the fifth emergency service. We know things. And we're local. On this estate I'd be on the scene much sooner than an ambulance or the police. I've delivered more babies than I can count and there were several local boys that I'd scared back onto the straight and narrow. I'd be no good in a fire, though, and no matter how cute your cat, you'd never find me up a tree.

"No." She'd frowned before answering. I could see her shadow-brow crinkle with concentration. I still couldn't work out who she was though. I nearly had it. I think she lived in the block but wasn't a client herself. A client's mother? A wife, maybe? I didn't know anyone who'd been widowed.

"Then why did you want to see me?"

"Bad man."

This made no sense.

"Bad ..." she paused, brow furrowed again. "Bad woman."

Bad man. Bad woman. What could that mean?

Unless ...

"Am I the bad woman?"

"Yes."

"Why?"

"Bad man."

The bad man made me a bad woman?

Oh no! The pieces fell together all at once. Her face became clear for the first time. I did know her!

"Veronica. You were going to see Jake when I was leaving him earlier. I thought you looked cross."

"Bad man."

"Wait! That was only an hour ago and he was fine then. When did you kill him?"

"Just now."

Typical! This was the one time when just now meant just now. Bloody ghosts!

I ran out the door and headed for the stairs that would take me down to Jake's flat. I could see Veronica's body in the courtyard below. How she had managed to fall over the balcony on the way up was a mystery, but it was one I couldn't be bothered with right now. Her ghost, now coloured properly, stood by the body and looked down at it mournfully.

Jake's flat was open – she hadn't bothered to close it in her mad dash to exact whatever twisted revenge she'd had in mind for me. As I charged in, I was already dialling for an ambulance. I knew that whatever I found would be beyond even my first-aid skills. I prayed I wasn't too late.

He was on the kitchen floor, a large pool of blood around his head and his favourite cast-iron frying pan on the floor beside him. He had a pulse, however. He was still alive!

"Bad man." She'd followed me in, but I ignored her while I finished calling for the ambulance.

"He's still alive," I said after I'd hung up. "You didn't kill him."

I crouched down beside him, getting Jake's blood on my dress. I didn't care.

"Bad man."

"No. He wasn't bad, Veronica. He loved you, but you were impossible to love. Impossible to please. You left him. Remember?"

"Bad man."

"Yes, you justified leaving him by saying he was bad. He was lazy, you said. He hit you, you said. He saw other women, you said."

"Bad –"

"No! You said that, but you were the bad one. You beat him. I saw the bruises. I saw him cooking and cleaning and washing dishes while you slept on the sofa surrounded by vodka bottles. He was too bloody knackered for other women. You probably put him off women for life."

I ignored her for a minute to make sure Jake was comfortable. The 999 operator had told me not to move him. I couldn't see anything to suggest a broken neck or a fractured skull, but I didn't want to take chances.

"Jake? Jake? Can you hear me?" He stirred but didn't wake. "It's Mags, love. I'm here. Don't worry, I've called an ambulance. They'll be here soon. Stay with me, won't you."

"I killed him."

"No, you didn't."

"Blood."

"Head wounds bleed a lot. You've hurt him, quite badly, but he's not dead."

She looked at me, confused. She didn't know what to do.

"You thought I was having an affair with him, didn't you?"

"Bad woman."

"Oh, bugger off. I saw him to fix his bruises and set his arm that one time when you hit him too hard." I looked down at him in the pool of his own blood. "That other time you hit him too hard. He was always too embarrassed to go to a doctor, so he got me to deal with his injuries. Then, when you left him, I came to rebuild his self-esteem, to tell him he wasn't the waste of air you said he was. I'm his friend."

"*Friend.*" She managed to say the word in italics. Sarcasm? From a ghost? She blinked at me.

"Yes, friend. You could have been his friend if you'd tried. Your marriage would have lasted longer if you had. I doubt you knew how to be anyone's friend. You attacked him for nothing, you hear? Nothing."

What was keeping her here? She knew now that she hadn't killed Jake and she thought she was in the right. She wouldn't want to apologise, and she didn't need my forgiveness.

I laughed then as the reason hit me. She still wanted me to admit I had been having an affair with her husband. She wanted to punish me the way she intended to when she was still alive.

"You wanted to hurt me, maybe kill me like you thought you'd killed Jake. That's why you were running."

She nodded slowly.

"And now you're dead and you blame me for that."

"Bad woman."

"You still want to kill me?"

She nodded again, and I laughed.

"Well, good luck with that, sister. You're a piss-poor ghost, you know that? You've hardly enough watts for me or any other witch to see you. You're never going to get enough strength to even touch me, let alone kill me."

Her lips pursed, and she glared at me.

"You know what? I'm going to let you stick around for a while to see if you can give yourself a break and move on. I know of at least seven ways to disperse a ghost and all of them are painful."

She looked smug at that point.

"Painful for the ghost. Notice I said I'd disperse you. I didn't say I'd help you pass over. I said disperse. Like a sugar lump in a cup of tea."

Her gloating smile faded as her fate became real to her. She knew she would be floating around me for a few years until I died or got pissed off with her.

I ignored her and reached over to grab Jake's hand and held it. I stroked his hair with my other hand as I waited for the blue lights to arrive.

PERFECT FLAVOUR

Nina Yakimiuk

Excited about the evening I chose a bright colourful dress. I picked the accessories to match with care. I wanted to look my best. This was a party I had anticipated with delight and I looked forward to seeing my friends.

When I arrived there were several people I knew. A table in the corner was spread with a lavish assortment of food. Macaroni salad, bread, green salad, chicken and various cheeses. I noticed the bread was pumpernickel (dark, hearty) and regular white. Next to it was a dish of smoked sausage and sauerkraut (Piekasch). Then I saw it...Borscht!

For years now I had stopped eating this red beet cabbage soup. My hostess Anna ladled a bowl for me. To my surprise it wasn't like the soup my mum used to make. "What kind of Borscht is this?" I asked.

Anna smiled and said, "Czech. Do you like it?". The perfect flavour made me think of my mother. To my delight I ate more and more. My hostess grinned. "Have some more," she said.

Just seeing the ethnic food made me glow with happiness and next morning I rang my mum. After a few greetings and light-hearted conversation I asked, "Do you have the recipe for Borscht?"

She gasped. "I though you hated it." I revealed how I had a surprise at Anna's party and said I wanted to try her recipe. She laughed and explained what ingredients I needed to buy. Also, she told me the steps of cooking it, so it would have that tangy taste. I also learned there are many ways to cook it depending which region of Ukraine you come from. Mum's recipe was from Poltava.

Giving it a go I realized that it took hours to cook. No wonder my mum made an enormous pot . . . enough to eat it every night for a week.

As I treated my friends to this soup memories came back. Trying to assimilate to the main culture I wanted to be more American than they were. The familiar dishes were abandoned for American food. Why this happened is something that puzzled me. Maybe it was because my parents clung to their traditions so much; national costumes, songs and heritage. They came to America but their hearts were in their native country. There is a saying. "Your feet are here in this country but your heart is in Ukraine." Another puzzle was what makes our identity? It is a feeling you belong to a group of people who share your traditions and everything that comes with it. Knowing the language and believing in the religion you grew up with and practicing it.

Then there is the dilemma of merging with the multitude. We lose something of ourselves and this wonderful heritage. If someone asked me "Where do you come from?" I would tell them that my parents come from Eastern Europe. I can explain with a smile my background plus the recipe for "Borscht".

MENTALLY ILL AND MENTALLY HAPPY TO REMINISCE

Fay Brown

Today I went to visit my aunt who is 89, has Alzheimer's and mental illness. For as long as I can remember she has been in and out of different care homes, and when very ill has been sectioned in the mental health section of her local hospital. In this case she is sectioned in a hospital in Chertsey because her care home refused to have her back after her recent breakdown.

The journey from Waterloo station was onerous – no direct train due to a rail strike so I had to get a train to Virginia Water and wait outside the "village like" station for a local bus to Chertsey Station. At Waterloo there was much hustle, bustle and colour – people pulling their suitcases, others queuing up to buy train tickets, some sitting down reading – but everyone keeping an eye on the large overhead screen to check what platform their train is leaving from. On the loudspeaker I hear "Reading Services" and within the list of stations "Virginia Water". I dash to platform 19 and decide to enter the middle of the train.

Sitting opposite me are a suntanned well-groomed elderly husband and wife, both holding Prêt a Manger disposable coffee cups and a paper carrier bag. I find out they are travelling to Ascot. The lady is very well dressed, nice earrings, coat and handbag. I begin to wonder where they got their suntan from, and assume they have recently returned from somewhere hot and expensive. Neither of them make eye contact with me which is interesting. I begin to imagine what kind of house they live in – large and detached with a driveway.

I ask myself why did I choose today to travel to visit my elderly aunt as the travel is so challenging? Even when I arrive at Chertsey station I will probably have to get a cab to the hospital. I've been told it's only a fifteen-minute walk to the hospital, but this is the countryside with many country lanes and dual carriageways. I'm already tired, but more importantly I need to think about my safety.

When I finally arrive at Chertsey, the local cab shop has a shabby door and it doesn't look like there's much action. I get chatting to the friendly driver who looks grateful for my booking. He tells me he used to work in London but has always lived in Chertsey, and that the cab shop has good business in the evenings and weekends due to commuters. He also says that many businesses have relocated from London to Chertsey due to high rent prices, and the local hotels are thriving from workers who "live" at the hotels during the week and go home to London at the week-end – what a reversal!

Back to aunty. I've arrived at the hospital and find the reception area deserted apart from a punky looking man with died pink hair, earrings in his nose and ears, and only one shoe on, and talking to himself in another language. I'm guessing he must be one of the outpatients. I remember telling the cab driver I am visiting my elderly aunt who is in her late 80's and has mental illness and Alzheimer's. He said *"that's not where an elderly lady should be staying, that's where drug users and addicts are kept, and sometimes I see them fighting outside"*

He had me thinking about my poor aunty having to stay in this place. When I pressed the buzzer to get access to her ward I felt like I was entering Fort Knox. Once inside I found a deserted corridor ahead of me with no directions. I felt like a trapped prisoner but thanked God when I noticed what looked like two staff members walking towards me. I asked directions to Spurgeon Ward. One said, *"You look very smart."*

Finally I found my aunty in the dining room with two members of staff. She looked like she'd put on weight, and stronger since the last time I saw her. She stared at me for several seconds before coming over, then we hugged, and she was so glad to see me. So what did I take away from my visit to aunty today?

- You must push the boat out when you have an elderly family member who's unwell with mental illness
- There are many people who are put in mental illness wards for different reasons – drug addiction, depression, violent behaviour, dementia or simply because the system doesn't have anywhere else to put them while they are deciding what to do.
- My aunty "lives" in a solitary room with very little possessions, a toothbrush, toothpaste, face cream, bed, a small wardrobe with a bare amount of clothes (I counted the number of garments on one hand).
- Every exit route in the department is locked, and even visitors cannot leave without a special exit button being remotely pressed.
- The outside world must have a "licence" to enter this world. I guess my licence is that I was a relative of an elderly "resident" in the mental health department.

What really touched me was despite the prison-like surroundings my aunt was happily reminiscing about her life in Jamaica when she was young, and that I was so happy to hear her wonderful memories. Not looking forward to the train journey back home to London though . . .

PUDDINGS AND PYES LAST GIG, 1979

Grahame Hood

It became obvious that not all was well between Fran and Mike. They had once been such a close couple, always affectionate in small ways. Fran eventually confided in Jenny.

"I just don't love him anymore, but the stupid thing is I don't know why. He's still the same Mike I fell in love with, but I must have changed. I just find him irritating. He's always so nice, I almost wish we could have a really good row and clear the air, but he always diffuses any tension. Maybe I should never have moved in with him and stayed with my parents a bit longer. If it's like this now, what will it be like when we are married? Maybe I'm not as grown-up as I thought I was?"

There was really nothing Jenny could say.

About two weeks later Jenny went upstairs to her room, thinking she was alone in the house. The bathroom door opened and Frances, naked, came out, looked in surprise and horror at Jenny and ran into Peter's bedroom. She left about half an hour later. Jenny turned on Peter.

"What the hell are you doing? What's Mike going to say? How long has this been going on?"

Peter tried to justify himself.

"She doesn't love him anymore. She hasn't for ages"

"What will this do to the band?"

"Mike doesn't have to know."

"Oh, I think he does!"

Nothing more was said. Later in the evening the phone rang. Peter knew who it was.

"That was Fran. She's told Mike."

"We've got a gig tomorrow night you know."

"Let's just try and get through it and have the shouting afterwards..."

Later, Jenny suggested to Peter that it might be wise to revise the set-list. "I was thinking particularly of not doing 'Long Black Veil'."

"Why?"

"Well, the plot, as I recall, is that a man gets hanged for a murder he didn't commit because he is too much of a gentleman to admit that he couldn't have done the murder because he was in bed with his best friend's wife at the time...though that's taking gentlemanly conduct a bit far, in my book."

"Good point," agreed Peter. "I think I'd better go through the song list now..."

Puddings & Pyes last gig was every bit as memorable as their first, though for different reasons. It was in the same club, too. It's fair to say there were tensions. Mike was well aware of Frances' feelings for Peter and the drive to the venue was silent, despite Jenny's efforts to smooth things over.

Peter was determined just to get through the gig, pick up their fee, and if it came to a fight in the car park afterwards, well, so be it. But they had to be professional with their music. They got three songs into the first half before Mike could stand it no longer. They had just finished Dylan's 'You Ain't Going Nowhere' when Mike snapped.

"You fucking prick!" he screamed at Peter. The audience's collective jaw dropped.

Mike's face was red, and tears were streaming down his face. He thought about punching Peter, he thought about pulling his guitar off him, and stomping on it, but he couldn't do it. He wasn't a fighter. He didn't even know how to punch. The room was in awestruck silence. He threw his guitar on the floor and screamed at the audience.

"And you're all a bunch of pricks too!"

He ran out of the club room. There were two minutes of uneasy silence before the club organiser took charge. "We'll have a short break now, I think. The band will be back in the second half. Let's have a round of applause!"

The room erupted in relieved clapping.

Jenny went to the car park, Where she found Mike sitting on the bonnet of his Mini. She made to hug him. He wouldn't let her.

"This is the end, isn't it Jen? The end of everything we worked for. All those great gigs when you woke up the next morning still singing, the best feeling ever. Those long drives back home, singing all the way. We were comrades, brothers and sisters in adversity. The four of us against a stupid, uncaring world. And your stupid prick of a brother and my stupid slag of a girlfriend have spoiled it. Spoiled it forever! I hate them!"

His tears were uncontrollable, and he was racked with sobs that came from the absolute depths of his being. She went to hug him again. This time, he let her.

"Sshh, Mike, it will be alright, it will. We can get another group together, just you and me, we'll be fine. Let it out. You'll feel better if you do."

She kissed the tears from his cheek. Peter and Frances watched them from the back door of the pub. After ten minutes or so Jenny felt Mike relax and his sobbing subsided. He looked her in the eye. Attempted a smile. She kissed him once, Mike aware of the taste of his own tears on her lips. Jenny walked back into the hall. Someone had picked up Mike's guitar and put it on the stage. It had a long scratch on the back from where he had thrown it on the floor. She picked it up, wiped it with a soft cloth, and put it in its case. She did the same with her banjo. Frances took her hand.

"I am so sorry Jen. So sorry. I've spoiled it for everyone."

Jenny forced a smile. "When it was good it was very, very, good wasn't it?"

Frances smiled back. Peter said nothing. He just looked embarrassed.

"Can you two get a lift back OK?"

"Yeah" said Peter. "Already sorted, see you later."

Jenny put her and Mike's instruments on the back seat of his Mini. He seemed OK to drive now.

"Take me home, Mike."

"You can stay with me if you want, Jen."

"No. Bad idea. Sorry. I really need to be alone in my own bed tonight."

They hadn't done the second half. The club organiser was understanding and gave them half their agreed fee, though they no longer cared. Puddings & Pyes never played again, and cancelled their remaining gigs.

Frances moved back in with her parents, and Peter started going to see her there. In time they became accepted as a couple, though Jenny still had mixed feelings about it, and was resentful of the fact that it had broken up the group. Nobody saw Mike for ages, though Jenny considered ringing him up to see how he was, before thinking the better of it. Peter and Frances seemed to lose their passion for music, and as far as Jenny knew, he had never even taken his guitar out of its case since the fateful night. Jenny started playing her banjo again, mainly in her bedroom. One pleasant summer evening she took it down to the bottom of the garden and sat on the step outside the shed, playing for what seemed like hours, with her eyes closed. She remembered the crowded rooms she had once played to. When she opened her eyes it was getting dark and the stars were coming out. She felt a deep sense of personal contentment and a great deal happier than she had for some time. She smiled, got up, and walked back into the house.

LOST PROPERTY

Carole Tyrrell

Judith was lost. To get away from the smiling man she'd taken what she thought was a short cut back to the car. Now she was alone in the narrow streets, her footsteps echoing off the cobbles, sweat making her t-shirt stick despite the late afternoon shadows.

"Where am I?" she thought after realising she had left the map behind in the cafe and that she didn't know Bruges as well as she thought. Judith paused for breath and glanced at a dusty chocolatiers window. The displayed goods were misshapen and mildewed. A middle-aged woman smirked at her after drawing back the lace curtain behind the display and then vanished behind it again as it dropped back. A cat washing itself on a doorstep paused and hissed, its back arched. Distracted, Judith tripped and fell heavily onto the cobble stones even though she put out her hands to stop herself. She was winded as one of her knees cracked onto the stone. The shoulder bag had spilled its contents all over the road and, momentarily dazed, she stared at them as if they were artefacts from an ancient civilisation. After a few moments, she managed to pull herself into a sitting position and rubbed her knee before reaching over to gather up her scattered possessions. The cat had trotted off on some mysterious feline errand and, as she watched it, Judith was suddenly conscious of the whole street becoming darker. The shade would have been welcome earlier in the day but now it felt as if it wanted to blot her out from the world. Taking a deep breath, she scrambled slowly to her feet and bent down to pick up her bag. "Oh no!" Judith muttered to herself as her favourite bracelet of glass beads caught on the bag's buckle and fell apart. The gleaming, tiny spheres fell onto the ground. As she painfully squatted down to retrieve them she saw a familiar figure at the end of the street in the gathering gloom. The beads forgotten, Judith hurried on again, feeling watched, sensing twitching curtains as she half-ran through the streets. But, as she turned a corner, she saw a line of stalls in the distance and, after pausing, gratefully walked towards them.

Judith felt safe within the throng of bargain hunters. "Silly to feel so frightened about going the wrong way. If I follow this line I'm bound to end up where I started from, and then I can get back to the car. Nothing will happen to me here, no-one would dare in the middle of all these people." The long line of stalls faded into a heat shimmer at the very end. But she felt cold.

*

It had been an impulse, a whim that had led her to Bruges. Judith had wanted to escape from her younger sister Alice's interminable wedding plans and had seen an offer on an online booking site.

"Sorry Judith, they can only do your fitting on Sunday morning. You don't mind, do you?" Alice had sounded contrite, but Judith wasn't convinced. The bridesmaid dress was a particularly unflattering colour on Judith and she had had enough of it all. So instead of visiting 'Brides R Us', she had booked her crossing two days earlier, boarded the Eurotunnel to Calais and kept driving until she arrived at Bruges. It had held happy memories for her as she and Dan had spent a blissful week there after university whilst traveling around Europe. They'd made plans which had fallen apart as soon as he met Alice on their return home. Now he was marrying Alice next month as if Judith and he had never been lovers.

"Was I the trial run?" she had once asked him, "Or was it Alice that you wanted all along?"

Dan had shrugged his shoulders. "It just happened at a party. She was there. I fancied her. Here we are."

Judith had always liked Bruges for its history and winding streets and had felt drawn to it as a refuge. The heat had hit her like a punch as she walked into town from the Minnewater car park. After a wet, rainy English summer she felt her senses unfurl again as the sun warmed her skin. She wandered into the vast August flea market and stood in the town square amazed at so many stalls and items for sale in one place. A four-foot tall crucified Christ lay on the ground as the bright sun made his silver painted loincloth glint. A gaggle of dressmaker's dummies stood clustered together as if in conversation whilst a group of naked female mannequins stared aloofly ahead as they struck a pose. Fox furs hung like laundry over the lid of an open suitcase, a Michelin man figure perched on a battered leather chaise longue and, on a table top, six crystal glass chandeliers glittered with tiny rainbows. Skeletal birdcages made of white painted wire resembled miniature Taj Mahals and gleamed like bone in the bright sunshine. A beautifully dressed statue of a female saint stood on a washstand and boxes of books gave some of the stalls a jumble sale air. Paintings carpeted some of the flagstones of the square and Judith almost trod on a copy of 'The Crying Boy'. Two carnival horses stood, frozen in mid gallop against a display of ephemera and Judith bent down to sift through the items. "Alice would be buying most of this to sell on eBay. Typical, she's always so clever." As she stood and looked at the haphazard collections of religious figures, handbags and garden furniture, she felt hemmed in by it all. There was too much to look at as her gaze darted like a butterfly. But in the midst of religious icons and imagery, as Judith idled along a side street, she came across a display of witch statuettes. "Ow!" she started as she felt a nip at her ankle. The dolls stared back at her, their resin faces gleefully gloating, long noses and long flowing synthetic white hair over their black costumes. Judith looked down at a statuette beside her and noticed a small spot of blood on her foot. A hand dived out of the tightly packed display and pulled the doll back into place again. Judith retreated into the bustling throng as it moved into a town square. But everyone was just looking and not buying. The market spread out in all directions and she began to feel nauseous. "It's that fish hanging up on that stall." She put her hand to her head and then walked towards a nearby café on the other side of the square. The iced coffee was cold and welcoming, and she felt revived as she took out her map.

The thump of a marching band, accompanied by cheers from the crowd, caught her attention. "It's like a carnival!" she thought as parents pointed out the bandsmen in their scarlet uniforms to their children. Judith's gaze wandered, and she noticed a small clean-shaven man dressed in a dark suit with a dark tie and a gleaming white shirt who stood on the opposite side of the street. He was smiling broadly and his brilliantined hair shone. Judith had the impression he was looking for someone. The band oom-pa pa'd past and as the drummer banged his drum with enthusiasm the man and Judith's eyes met. She looked away as the other customers raised their glasses in salute, but when she glanced back from the corner of her eye she saw him watching her. "He's looking for me!" Judith thought, knowing that it wasn't possible. Nobody knew that she was here, and she'd left no note. A text had come from Alice demanding to know what she thought she was up to and that she would never forgive her. Judith had deleted it immediately. "It's absurd. Why would a complete stranger be looking for me?" Goose pimples broke out on her skin. She couldn't explain it but on a deeper level she knew that he'd found her, and she shivered. She looked back but he was gone, and she breathed a sigh of relief. The bandsman with the big drum brought up the rear and a small group of children marched along in imitation. She summoned the waiter for the bill and, after paying, picked up her shoulder bag to leave. A group entering the cafe jostled her and she had to pause to collect herself. When she turned around the smiling man was before her.

Judith froze, feeling trapped.

"Madam -" he began in a deep and cultured voice. She turned and almost ran, clutching her bag to her chest whilst making her escape around tables and diners, apologising as she went, half-jogging along the street back towards the car park.

"It's ridiculous, how could he possibly know me?" She decided to take a different route from the one she had intended, and let herself be absorbed into the crowd.

*

There seemed to be even more people in the part of the flea market she had just entered. She heard the drum thumping in the distance as she thought she recognized the street and relaxed, feeling that she was no longer lost. "Silly to be frightened of a complete stranger. He just mistook me for someone else. I'll follow this line back to the train station and then I'll be back at the car." She checked her watch. There was still plenty of time. As she idly looked over a stall a familiar object attracted her attention. "I had one of those before Alice took it." Judith couldn't resist picking up the little Snoopy doll dressed in its little sweatshirt and jeans. On impulse she lifted its top and saw written in childish writing, 'Mine Judith.' "How much?" she asked the stallholder.

"Madam, it's yours." replied the middle-aged woman in a faded print summer dress pausing in mid-bite of her sandwich. Judith thanked her and, feeling uneasy, moved on, having put the Snoopy doll back on the stall. She let herself be carried along to the next one which was piled with dog-eared books. Most of them were Flemish and French titles including one TinTin adventure and she found some English titles amongst them. 'Alice in Wonderland', 'Flower Fairies of the Seasons', and 'Little Grey Rabbit.' She smiled at memories of reading them as a child. A momentary breeze blew one book open and she saw written on the flyleaf, 'To dear Judith, Happy Birthday, much love Nan and Grandpa.' Judith's hand went automatically to her bracelet of glass beads, but it was no longer there, and her hand twisted around her wrist instead. "Just coincidence that's all. Happens all the time," she thought, as she looked at the bright blue sky.

"Did you want something Madam?" asked the man behind the counter.

"No, no, just looking," said Judith as she began to turn away.

"But Madam, let me give you a book for your journey home". The owner came out from behind his stall and she felt something being put in her bag as it swung from her shoulder.

"I don't want to buy anything!" she almost shouted, and turned around to remonstrate, but he was back in his place, staring at her. She turned back in the direction from which shed come but was pushed and pulled by invisible hands moving her away from the train station and the car.

A push in the small of her back almost made her fall and she clutched onto a stall for support. Someone had trodden on her toes with force and they throbbed along with her knee. She saw the smiling man again as she looked around for somewhere to sit. He was standing behind the tables in front of some parked cars and a broad strip of grass. Families picnicked on either side of him at a distance.

"I've got to get back; I'll miss my sailing otherwise!" She glanced down at her watch and saw it was no longer on her wrist. Judith's hair hung in damp strands on her forehead as she clutched her bag again and tried to use it as a battering ram to push her way through the crowd. But they, all jostling elbows and knees, and stamping feet, spat her out at another collection of well used toys. "That's my stuffed rabbit." Judith muttered, and her fingers reached out to trace the patched hole where their dog had chewed it. The stallholder was fanning himself with a magazine, but she felt his eyes on her. As she was carried along the line by the swell of strangers she saw more treasured possessions that had vanished over the years. "Where am I?"

"Would Madam like some jewellery?" The smiling man was displaying a silver charm bracelet before her. She drew back and felt sick as she recognized the hedgehog, the Scottie dog, the clown.

"No, no it's not mine!" she shouted. He replaced it on the pile of entwined necklaces and beads where it gleamed in the fading sun. She wanted to run far away but his eyes held her, dark, fathomless, black.

"Who said that it was yours Madam? What are you looking for? Maybe I can help you?" She heard a faint accent in his voice.

"I don't know. I never did." she said slowly. He indicated by a wave of his hand that she should move on. She was on the verge of crying in utter frustration as she looked for an escape route, but found herself surrounded by people's backs. If she attempted to move in any direction except forwards they moved to block her way. She felt as powerless as a child. No one else was looking at the items on sale and, as she continued to look around, Judith realised that she couldn't see any faces. They were always turning away or looking in another direction and she began to feel glad that she couldn't see them.

"Beatrice! It's Beatrice!" The group of Victorian dolls, dressed in their Sunday best, were arranged sitting around a doll sized table with a small doll's tea set placed before them. Beatrice was the largest and the others were seated around her in order of size. Judith had always felt that it was their disturbingly realistic replica human eyes that had always made them look so creepy, as if a real human child was trapped inside a body of clay. Beatrice had been a family heirloom; first her grandmother's, then her mother's, and finally Judith's. She had lived in the glass fronted cabinet in the lounge until Judith could be trusted to play with her. She couldn't wait as none of her friends had a doll like Beatrice, and she had loved her. Then the nightmares had begun. "But her mouth is open!" thought Judith, "and the teeth are pointed! Just like in my dreams." She closed her eyes and when she looked back Beatrice's mouth was closed in an enigmatic half-smile. "She's watching me again Mum!" Judith had said to her mother once too often after the nightmares, and Beatrice had gone from the cupboard. Now she was at the centre of the group.

"Ah, Madam, you recognise her, and she recognises you." said a familiar voice beside her. The smiling man was at her side and she felt compelled to look at him. "Come with me, I have many other things to show you."

"He's not smiling at all," she finally realised. The grin was merely a rictus as his eyes remained cold. "I've got to get back, I'm meeting someone," she began to gabble as he seized her wrist.

"But Madam, no one knows you are here." The grip was firm, he was in control. He began to lead her forward and she shouted but no-one seemed to notice.

As they reached the high wall at the end of the street, the crowd parted to let them through and then reformed as if they had never been part of it. "I've been washed up like driftwood." He held her wrist tightly as he pushed open the huge wooden door set into the wall. A large arch encircled it and as she was led through the open doorway she saw cherubs carved into the doorframe. They smirked at her and one was putting out his tongue. Judith and the man emerged into a large open courtyard with a red brick house behind it, its shuttered windows making it look half asleep. A small fountain, its water tinkling, was at the centre of the yard with a carved border of florid roses along its outer edges.

"Are you part of the flea market?" she asked as he released her before a semi-circle of twelve stalls and their owners. The sun shone on a small pile of glass beads on the one nearest to her.

"Madam, we are the other flea market. We deal with precious things here. Things that were once precious to their owners and to whom we want to return them." She turned to look at him as he spoke.

"But Beatrice, my mother gave her away. She wasn't prec -"

"She wanted to be reunited with you Madam, and after all, what harm could it do?"

Judith turned again, hoping to run back to the door before it was closed. But where the doorway had been there was now only a blank wall in its place.

"Madam we have done our part now you must do yours."

"I have to go! I don't want the book, you can have it back!" Judith fumbled in her bag but the book had gone. "I've got some Euros, take them instead!" She began to gabble as she threw the notes at him. He ignored them, and a gust of air swept them into the fountain. Judith felt raindrops on her face which mixed with the tears beginning to form at the corners of her eyes.

"Judith we will only accept the most precious thing that you possess." With a shock she realized that they had been waiting for her all the time. Judith sank to her knees.

She managed to summon up the strength to shout as thunder began to roar.

"Why me?"

"Why not you?" he said as the sellers came out from behind their empty tables and advanced towards her. She thought that she could hear herself screaming for help until the rain began to thunder down, drowning her cries as the smiling man and his companions surrounded her.

RULES FOR WRITING GROUPS AND HOW TO RUN THEM

Heather Johnston

Ooh. (Sucks teeth). Search me. If you find out, let me know.

Actually, there are no rules for writing groups, and there is a reason. The great William Goldman once said, when asked how to write a successful script for Hollywood (pardon me while I go into capitals) 'NOBODY KNOWS'.

Nobody knows which book/story/script/poem/graphic novel will catch the imagination of the public or - more to the point when you're starting out - the attention of an agent or publisher. Certainly, 'nobody knows' which work written today, let alone published today, will be regarded an earth-shattering literary classic a few decades down the line. Or which huge success of today will fade away like Dracula at dawn. Sir Walter Scott was once the most popular novelist in all of Europe.

Because 'nobody knows', there's no point in worrying about it. The task of a writing group is not to reveal literary classics of the future, it's to get you blighters hitting the keyboard (all right, picking up a pencil, for the Luddites) and actually writing some stuff. Any stuff. Whatever you like. Don't be constrained by what your old English teacher would think- write what you think and how you express yourself today. Even grammar and form change radically over time, or we'd all still be writing Chaucerian rhyming couplets.

First, a few pointers. For the sake of the sanity of any agent/publisher/Steven Spielberg who may get to read what you write, there are some elements of what can be called writer's hygiene. These are in the 'boring but essential' box, and come with practice.

Spelling matters. Learn how to use the spell-check. Invest in a good dictionery (see what I did there?). Bad spelling is simply annoying and looks slipshod. If you are dyslexic, get a friend to help.

Basic grammar matters although in creative writing, you have more freedom than if you were drafting a legal document. If your grammar is getting between you, your meaning and your reader/audience, change the grammar. If you need guidance, buy a copy of Fowler's Modern English Usage.

Get used to writing in standard layouts, as changing afterwards is a BIND. Most publishers, competitions, agents etc. look for a clearly set-out, double-spaced document in 12-point font, Arial (in Europe) or Times New Roman or Courier (in the US). Agents for novels and stories look for paragraphing without an empty line between, with the first line inset - unless they say otherwise. Don't use a business layout, it grates on them. Don't use bullet points. Plays and scripts have layout conventions, which you can find on the BBC Writersroom website.

These conventions are so that the professional readers at theatres, publishers, agents, or TV companies can read through many, many manuscripts without tripping over some bizarre layout that makes their life difficult. Your creativity is in your work, not your typeface.

Most work is submitted electronically these days, which means a Microsoft Office Word document, RTF or a pdf. Digitisation marches on. Don't expect anyone to wade through your handwriting.

ALWAYS KEEP A COPY.

ALWAYS BACK UP.

Right. Now stare at a blank wall for a few days - or months.

Er, no.

One of the striking things about writers, especially the famous ones, is how much they write. They write lots. We may only remember a poem about daffodils, but Wordsworth's works extend to seven volumes. Even Keats, dead at twenty-six, wrote several volumes of poems, plays, essays and letters. Emily Bronte has only one published novel to her name, but the 'juvenilia' that she composed with Bramwell and her sisters is vast.

You don't get to write lots by waiting for divine inspiration nor by trying to perfect every line. You don't get to write lots by being afraid. You don't get to write lots by worrying if what you write makes you look like a bad person, or your mother won't approve, or it's just too weird, or it makes you reveal things within your mind and body that you have never really wanted to look at very closely.

Actually, none of that matters, anyway. It's all just marks on a page - or pixels on a screen. If you don't like it, you can throw it away. You should not throw it away because it makes you afraid, however. You can throw it away if it is clunky beyond remedy, or stops rather than ends, or wanders off, or would not be understood by someone other than yourself. Oddities can succeed - look at Tristram Shandy by Laurence Sterne, or Ubu Roi by Alfred Jarry. If you write lots, the weird stuff will find its own place. (And remember, if you're Stephen King, it could make you rich.)

Joining a writing group can be very helpful, because it reassures you that there are other weirdoes out there just like you. Be aware that groups can be cliquey

- if you run one, avoiding this is a permanent problem. Some spend more time attacking each other than critiquing work. Or the group is terribly nice, listens to work in respectful silence, and tells the writer how wonderful they are - which is equally useless. Like any interest group, you need to match the characters of the members as well as their interests.

Striking out boldly, I have set myself some rules for the group I've been caretaking for about eight years.

Rule one is that I don't know. If I did, I'd be running Bloomsbury Publishing, and I'm not. So my word is not final, although I do try to inspire and facilitate discussions. I don't mark work, either: competent writers must learn to judge their own stuff, as this is not school. You don't get to be a writer by passing exams.

Rule two is that we're here to help. 'Criticism' has developed a negative association, but in order to assess how successfully writing communicates, we need to critique it. Critiquing means looking at it in detail to see what works and what does not, and suggesting how it might be changed to work better. Any piece of writing can be made to work better. For the intellectual underpinning for this kind of 'criticism', read Matthew Arnold, who goes into why we need critics and what they should aim to do.

Rule three is a corollary: whether the group 'like' a piece is not very important - nor if we 'dislike' a piece. We do not run Bloomsbury, either. We can only say how it affects us and what we get out of it, and match that to the writer's intentions. Does it work?

Rule four: you can write ANYTHING - you won't shock me. I used to joke that I did not care if the group write pornography, and everyone would laugh in embarrassment. And then 'Fifty Shades of Grey' came along and made someone very rich indeed.

Rule five: the acid test for writing is to show it to someone else. The one certain way of knowing what you should have done is to send a piece to a competition, because before the email hits their in-box, all your terrible mistakes and sheer amateurishness will rise before you like Marley's ghost. Another way is to read work out to a group. This really works - not on them, on you. I'd say it's vital. But often excruciating.

Rule six: be prepared to talk about your work. Many writers are truly terrible at this. They look at you like a baby seal about to be clubbed, and mutter. Or gape. But as I've heard a writer say, 'Shy girls get no broth' (she is a Scot). Your genius needs to be escorted confidently into the world, not abandoned on a doorstep.

So what should writers write?

Rule seven: if I could, I would ban the words 'should' and 'ought'. Writing is about you, not what other people expect.

Writers are best when they are themselves. As Oscar Wilde put it, 'Be yourself. Everyone else is already taken.' Why be a pale and inaccurate imitation when you can be the real deal?

At this point, a word of caution. You may have a Vital Message for the World but as another favourite critic of mine, Sam Goldwyn, once said, 'Messages are for Western Union'. It is an unfortunate truth that high intentions alone do not deliver high art. If we aim to be 'high' because only that is 'serious' we must navigate between kitsch, tedium, sheer ineptitude and a kind of frantic over-finishing because serious stuff needs lots of weird long words and metaphors and things.

Or we can find our own way of talking to our reader or audience, and refine that to simplicity, clarity and power.

Our subject, what we talk about, is up to us. But writers are more than cameras. Writers observe, but they also construct, and every writer, consciously or unconsciously, constructs and expresses a moral viewpoint when they write. However, the best writers don't shout about their moral positions: they express them through the characters and actions in their writing.

Matthew Arnold has a good phrase in 'The Study of Poetry': writing is 'a criticism of life', by which he meant the application of ideas to life. Ideas alone are not enough: they must be tested by real experience. But experience alone is not enough, either, because without ideas, that is simply a puddle of sensations. To go out and publicly commit to a moral position, to critique life, does take some personal courage: Arnold quotes Heinrich Heine, a writer who saw himself as 'a brave soldier in the Liberation War of humanity'.

Those may seem rather lofty descriptions, as you hack away at your piece on how your primary teacher destroyed your artistic confidence, or your sci-fi epic about mutant guinea pigs. But the power of writing, the creative impulse to experience, analyse, synthesize and then communicate, is what matters, whether you are Homer, Joanna Trollope, Shakespeare, Jane Austen or PG Wodehouse. Or, indeed, Mark Gatiss, J.K. Rowling, or Guillermo Del Toro.

So be brave enough to say your piece, and find a group brave enough to listen to you. And then be brave enough to take constructive criticism, and use it to make your writing work better.

And then send it out. But that's another story -

ABOUT THE AUTHORS

Fay Brown was born in London and has lived for most of her life in the inner city. She has a great empathy for people affected by stereotypes and social issues, and through her writing challenges the status quo. She is inspired by her work with vulnerable and disadvantaged people through her extensive years of working in local government and the charity sector.

Ian D. Brown is a proud South Londoner and keen sport's observer who smashes the myth that 'what happens in the locker room stays in the locker room' and lifts the lid on the unseen toxic and sometimes brutal world of an intense football dressing room at half-time. Ian briefly submerges the reader in the sights, sounds and complex relationships of the characters to what is commonly referred to as the 'beautiful game', that in essence is anything but.

Ana Castellani has poetry published in the anthologies Lost Things and Mad Like Us. Her work has existentialist and philosophical flavours, and is fuelled by a keen interest in neuroscience and psychology. When not travelling around the world to save the financial industry Ana relaxes by watching TV, singing, dancing and driving around the gorgeous county of Kent.

R.E. Charles has many publications to his name, his most critically acclaimed being *Diary of a Man Who Thought He Was A Splintered Toothpick in a Paris Café During the One Hundred Year War (the teabag years) Part VI.* Charles has been the recipient of several awards, including *Best Nineteen-Seventies Haircut* (which he won in 2013), and *Turd of the Year* at *Modern Woman Magazine's* annual awards, for which he suffered the mis-judgement of actually turning up to receive.

Samantha Edwards has written for as long as she can remember. Whether in the form of song, poetry or social commentary, her work is true to her natural thoughts and feelings. She loves life, people and rainbows, and hopes it shows on paper.

Cleo Felstead grew up in Middlesex and now lives in North Kent with her partner and 2-year-old son. Always feeling freed by the pen, she flirts with the idea of writing on a regular basis and actually writes something occasionally. A full-time mum and part-time children's DJ, Cleo spends a lot of time playing musical statues and splashing in muddy puddles.

Tia Fisher writes prose and poetry for both younger and older adults. Poems have previously been published in *The Rialto* magazine; she has won a *'Tubeflash'* competition and been longlisted for the *MsLexia Children's Book Award.* She is currently working on a YA narrative verse novel. Tia lives in Kent, where she deprives husband, cats and teenagers of attention in order to write.

Trish Gomez lives in south London and enjoys the theatre, cinema and reading historical fiction, nonfiction and mystery novels. She has had success in a Woman's Weekly short story competition and had a story published in a magazine. *The Grey Lake* combines Trish's love of history with that of a good mystery.

Dominic Gugas lives in Kent as the lone male with his partner, two daughters and two cats. He works in technology for a bank and spent much of his career designing call centres, which may make him one of the most evil beings on the planet. When he is not unleashing technological terrors on the public Dominic writes stories in the historical, fantasy, science fiction and "office weird" genres. The V Plan Diet is his first published work.

Edna Herbert loves writing and uses this creative gift to inspire, encourage and provoke her audience. Her work varies from inspirational words of encouragement to social commentary.

Grahame Hood was born in Peebles, 20 miles south of Edinburgh. He has lived in the Bromley area since the late 1970's, and worked as a Civil Servant before being offered early retirement which he was more than happy to accept. He plays many acoustic folk music instruments and has written a full-length book, many articles, CD sleeve notes and reviews on the subject, his particular niche interest being in what could broadly be called "British progressive folk music 1969-1973." He is currently co-writing (with a former RE teacher) a novel called 'The Pudding Papers' which he hopes has the makings of a Radio 4 cult comedy series, an extract from which is included here.

Heather Johnston writes plays for theatre, novels and short stories. Three one-act comedies have been performed professionally in London fringe theatres, and she has written four full-length plays. Recently Heather has concentrated on novels (4) and a sequence of 15 short stories, of which 2 have been published to date. Born in County Durham and brought up in South-East London, Heather read English at Oxford University, and has qualifications in economics and statistics. After working in advertising, marketing and business consultancy, Heather is currently a freelance consultant.

Jeannine Lehman is a former banker living and writing in London. She grew up in the United States and her father was indeed an American football coach, which left her with a love of the game. She travels the world extensively and loves to read good books.

Gwynneth Pedler was born in the East End of London in 1925, before moving to Maidenhead at the beginning of World War 2 and then later to Oxford, though she has now moved back to London to be near her two daughters. She had a long career in teaching, the last 15 years as a Head teacher. After retirement she went to Poland, which had just achieved independence, to teach English for 7 years, then to the same situation in Albania. These experiences were the inspiration for this story; she has ideas for more stories based on her adventures. Following a road traffic accident she now relies on a wheelchair for mobility. She is well known for her ardent campaigning for equality, independence and accessibility. She loves children, cats, her garden and wearing bright clothes; dislikes pompous people. She is a practising Christian who thinks Churches don't laugh enough. Her next piece of prose will be "Where has all the laughter gone?" based on passages in the Bible that mention laughter.

Siobhan Reardon is an Irish writer living in London. She loves: laughing loudly, the burnt end of bread, seeing the white plumes of her own breath on a frosty January morning and the sight of spring lambs jumping in the fields of Kent. Her list of dislikes has been carefully edited and shoved away in a draw for now, and she is fascinated by the themes of everyday life and what underpins it, and how memory leaves its ghostly imprint on our lives.

Loraine Saacks arrived on this planet, in London, a few days after Pearl Harbour was attacked, and enjoyed Anderson Shelters, travelling on the underground and seeking refuge in Chislehurst Caves. She still feels happier underground than aloft. Had a few lines published in *Mslexia* Issue 63, in 2014, one short story read on *Bromley (YDN) Radio* in 2015, one poem published in Live Cannon's '*154 Poems By 154 Contemporary Poets in Response to Shakespeare's 154 Sonnets*', in 2016, one short story shortlisted by *Writers' and Artists' Year Book Competition* in 2016, and several poems in '*Croydon Poetry Hour*' 2016-2017 and 2017- 2018 Anthologies. Currently being re-booted, as an au pair for late arrival of flurry of grandchildren. Addicted to Lidls, rubber bands, one-pan cooking, off-piste cinema, Yesterday, PBS America and Smithsonia television channels, BBC1 television's *'Question Time'* and Radio 4's *'The Archers'*. Neither a bird nor a modern music lover, but very fond of Giraffes and Elephants.

Simon Thompson, a failed classicist who now spends his time working with data, is obsessed with the themes of recurrence and number patterns. "Four Themes on Summer" draws on this, pulling together four remembered and significant moments in his life. He is currently working on complementary pieces of the topics of Winter, Spring and Autumn.

Carole Tyrrell has always been fascinated by the supernatural and the weirdness of everyday life. Lost Property was inspired by a day trip to the legendary Bruges flea market where she did find and buy a Snoopy doll and wondered what might happen if she discovered more lost childhood treasures . . . Carole is also intrigued by the growth in Folk Horror and hopes to take part in the re-scouring of the Uffington White Horse again. She has been published in Enigmatic Tales, The Silent Companion, Ghosts & Scholars and more recently in A Ghost and Scholars Book of Folk Horror.

Robert Williams has written two pieces for this anthology, both about an urban witch called Mags who lives in a flat in South East London. By a strange coincidence, Robert also lives in a flat in South East London, but he isn't a witch. As well as writing, Robert likes photography, holidays and quirky science fiction shows. He's currently working on more Urban Witch stories.

Nina Yakimiuk attends the Brixton Creative Writing Group and has work in both the poetry and prose sections of South of the River. Perfect Flavour is influenced by her Eastern European roots.

ABOUT THE EDITOR

Raymond Little is a Londoner who now lives in Kent. He has personal links with both Bromley and Brixton, which made the editing of this anthology a project very close to his heart. His short stories have appeared in many anthologies including the resurrected *Horror Library* series and Blood Bound Book's *DOA II* and *Night Terrors III. The End of Science* was a Dark Tales prize winner and was published in CEA's Greatest Anthology. He was included in the Dead End Follies article *10 Brilliant Writers You Probably Don't Know*, and his story *An Englishman in St. Louis* sat alongside some of his own literary heroes such as Dickens, Poe and Conan Doyle in the *Chilling Ghost Short Stories* collection. His debut novel, *Eyes of Doom*, was published in 2017, and his novella *Love Kills* was released in 2018, under the pen-name R.E. Charles. Forthcoming works include the novel *Thin Places* and an anthology of his own horror short stories, and he is currently working on his novel *The South London Trilogy. South of the River* is Ray's debut as an editor.

Read more about Ray's work at raymondlittle.co.uk.

40583025R00094

Printed in Poland
by Amazon Fulfillment
Poland Sp. z o.o., Wrocław